THE OLD MAN IN A STATE HOUSE

& Other Stories

THE OLD MAN IN A STATE HOUSE

& Other Stories

by

TANURE OJAIDE

AFRICAN HERITAGE PRESS
New York • *Lagos* • *London*

AFRICAN HERITAGE PRESS

NEW YORK
PO BOX 1433
NEW ROCHELLE, NY 10802
USA

LAGOS
PO BOX 14452
IKEJA, LAGOS
NIGERIA

TEL: 914-481-8488 / 855-247-7737
FAX: 914-481-8489
customerservice@africanheritagepress.com
www.africanheritagepress.com

First Edition, African Heritage Press, 2012

Library of Congress control number: 2011941392

Ojaide, Tanure

Cover Design: Dapo Ojoade
Cover Art: Dr. Bruce Onobrakpeya

ISBN: 978-0-9790858-7-1
ISBN: 0-9790858-7-x

Again, in memory of Grandma Amreghe

Contents

CHAPTER ONE

The Benevolence
of the Dead

MY FATHER'S FIRST VISIT TO me from the dead was when I lived with my uncle, his younger brother. He had left two of us, me, a girl, and my brother, who was taken by my aunt. I did not understand what informed my going to my uncle and my brother going to my aunt. Maybe we were shared on the basis of seniority, since I, the elder child, went to Uncle while Auntie, junior to him, took my younger sibling. Our mother was too young and still at Isiokolo Teachers' Training College and could not provide for us; hence we had to be shared between my father's brother and sister.

Either my uncle did not know how to take care of a child or he was wicked and must have been one of my father's relatives who caused his untimely death. He was not yet married and taught in a secondary school at Ughelli. He did not believe in always having food in the house. He only asked for food to be prepared at very late hours after hunger had almost knocked me out.

I did not eat in the morning before I went to school and did not have lunch too. By the time our school closed, I was already half-fainting from hunger but managed to drag myself back to the house. It took time before I was asked to prepare dinner. It appeared my uncle ate outside and did not care about me. If he did not eat outside and felt hungry as I did, there would have been food in the house all the time. He was robust and his stomach continued to grow big. Sometimes when he spoke to me, I could smell the aftertaste of beer which he drank outside but never at home. After this had gone on for quite some time, I had to collect palm kernels and *kpokpo* garri to eat to check my constant hunger. I hid these "foodstuffs" in my schoolbag so that my uncle would not know that I was fighting hunger in my own way. I feared that if he saw me he might seize and throw them away to keep me hungry.

On weekends, we went to the farm where my uncle planted yams. We did not eat before leaving for the farm and ate when we returned in the hot afternoon. I thought I was going to die from the unrelenting torture of hunger. My school uniform hung over my emaciated body. I started to pray that God should give me food. I knew that if my father had not died, I would not be hungry. It was that night, after my prayer, as I slept or was half-asleep, that my father stepped in and stood by the threshold of my bedroom. Though I closed the bedroom door before I went to bed, I did not know how it opened.

"Don't be afraid," he told me.

I was scared despite his assurance. I knew he was long dead. The dead had a different demeanor from the living. His clothes, though like what he used to wear, appeared weird and rumpled. The color was faded but the same light blue that he used to like wearing.

"You will be fine," he said.

He had tears running from his eyes, perhaps shocked that I had emaciated so much and was always hungry. He stood there and gazed at me for a while and occasionally shaking his head. His eyes shone like stars far in the sky. He then turned away and left. When I came to myself, or rather woke up, the bedroom door had shut itself as before I went to bed.

The following day I had my first good meal for a long time. My mother came to visit and brought two big loaves of bread and corned beef. The following day I had breakfast and lunch of bread and corned beef. In the evening, as if to give the impression of normalcy in the house, my uncle asked my mother to prepare egusi soup with beef and stockfish, which we ate with *eba*. Mother did not know that this dinner was unusual, but I could not tell her that I was constantly hungry before now. I hoped, but was not convinced, that after my mother left I would now be having egusi soup and *eba* at least once a day. But as soon as she left, the daily routine of torture at the hands of hunger started again.

My uncle did not want to send me to a secondary school. It was not that he did not have the means to do so, but for reasons I could not understand. I saw secondary school girls in their white and brown checkered uniforms, and I liked them. I wanted to go to school so that I would become neat and smart like them. I also wanted one day to become a teacher. I had got money from my aunt—when she visited—to pay for the Common Entrance Examination, after my father had paid me another visit. I passed and was admitted to St. Mary Magdalene Girls' Secondary School at Ashaka. Instead of congratulating me for passing, my uncle scolded me for taking the entrance examination without telling him beforehand. If I had told him, I would not have registered for the entrance examination, not to talk of passing and getting admitted into the school.

Late in the evening, as my uncle sat in his favorite cushion chair in the sitting room to relax, I told him about my admission to the girls' secondary school.

"I don't have the money for you to go to school," he told me categorically.

"What do you want me to do after elementary school?" I asked.

"All I know is that there is no money. There is plenty of land around to farm," he said.

"Uncle, I don't want to farm. I want to go to a secondary school and read books," I pleaded.

"Are you deaf?" he thundered.

He slapped me by the right ear that became numb with pain. I cried and cried but there was nobody to listen to me. My uncle had banged the door and left the house. That night my father visited again. This time I was not scared like the previous times. His eyes still shone like stars in the sky and his voice husky as in earlier times, but he was himself calm.

"Don't argue with your elders if it will not help," my dead father counseled.

This time I replied.

"Yes, I won't henceforth, Daddy!"

"You will go to school. Don't worry. Continue to read till the time comes. When you go to school, don't let anything distract you from your studies. Help your uncle in the farm so that he will not beat you again," he said.

He did not wait for me to respond to his advice before he turned and walked away through the main door of the house. Always walking backwards and disappearing into thin air after a short while.

I wanted to help my uncle in the farm with all my energy, as I had promised my father. I expected my uncle to change his mind and agree to send me to the secondary school. If I could go to secondary school, I would read and read and not be distracted by anything. I had made the promise to my father and would not break it.

Two weeks later, a university friend of my father visited. Mr. Tony Bedebede had looked for my mother and us, the children. When my mother told him about my passing the entrance examination to the secondary school and her not being able to send me there, he shook his head in pity, bit his lips, and told my mother not to worry.

"I can take care of that for my friend's sake," he said.

He came to visit my uncle with the singular purpose of seeing me. My uncle had gone out that evening when Mr. Bedebede visited. "You look so much like your dad. I hope you will be as intelligent as he was," he told me, caressing my shoulder. I shook my head in response because I did not know what to tell him. That was not the first time that I had been told that I looked like my father. As for his intelligence, I wanted to be my father's daughter in appearance and intelligence. "Your uncle must be taking good care of you," Mr. Bedebede said, "so you are sure of your upkeep for now. I will help you with your secondary school as I have promised your mother."

When my uncle came home and I told him that Mr. Bedebede, my father's friend, had come to visit, he did not appear to be happy because he did not ask me anything about him.

The following day Mr. Bedebede went to the school to pay three years' tuition fees on my behalf. Tony Bedebede would pay my school fees and even give me pocket money on a regular basis for the rest of my secondary school education.

I wanted to live with my mother after my secondary school, but I was ordered to remain with my uncle. The same problem of school fees came up when I wanted to go to the university. I had gained admission to the University of Benin to study Geography, which I so much liked. My father had graduated with a Bachelor's degree in Geography and had liked the subject so much, I had learned from my mother. Why I so much liked the subject myself I did not know. But I was very happy that I had been admitted to study Geography.

The problem of money arose immediately. My mother only had a Teachers' Grade Two Certificate and could barely take care of herself. She was lucky that she lived and taught at Ughelli and so did not pay any rent with my father's house left for her. She had been surprised that the wicked relatives who killed my father, according to her, did not strip the house of my father's property or take the house from her. She told me that none of them would have survived a night in the house since my father's ghost would have either killed them or driven them crazy. In any case, it would not be possible for my mother to pay my fees while in the university, even if she was to starve. Her pay was paltry and would not go anywhere towards meeting her needs and mine at school. I was worried and started crying, feeling helpless after being admitted into the university.

Again, true to his watchful nature, my father visited me that night when I was distressed.

"Don't worry. You'll be fine," he said.

This time he smiled; his teeth were brown as if he had been chewing kola nuts since he died. He stepped forward wanting to pat my hair, but some force immediately pulled him back, as if he was about to do a forbidden thing. He stepped back from me and walked with his back away, his words of encouragement echoing in the night air. Only I must have heard the loud words. *Don't worry. You will be fine. You will be fine. You will be fine. Always remain a good girl. . .*

A cousin of ours, who had been friendly with my father, worked in Ethiope Bank. Mr. John Uvie got to know of my admission to study Geography with neither my mother able nor my uncle ready to pay my school fees. Surprisingly, he promised to take care of me while in the university. And true to his word, Mr. Uvie was a great guardian while I was studying, and I fared much better financially than many students who had fathers and mothers. I could not complain but only thanked God for his mercies. I promised myself to remain the good girl that my father expected of me at least until after I had graduated and started to work. I also realized that at least one of my father's relatives, a distant one, was not wicked. My mother did not mean the like of Mr. Uvie when she talked about my father's relatives.

In my final year at the university, I had a boyfriend. I had wanted to face my books and not to get distracted by any relationships before then. However, Ogaga was a very intelligent and smart young man. After we started to study together, preparing for tests and examinations, I fell deeply in love with him. I could not resist his charm, but I held back from being intimate with him as long as I was a student. I wanted to do very well in my exams to please my guardian and also my father. After all, they would be disappointed if I did not do well. I always felt that my father was watching me as I studied.

My father did not visit before my final exams. I was worried because I expected him to cheer me up before I started writing. Maybe he felt I was ready and did not need further assistance. He had always visited me when I had difficulties that I could not solve by myself. I guessed he knew that I could cope with my final exams if I worked hard and I was not distracted; hence he chose not to visit me at the time. At some stage, I blamed myself for expecting my dead father, who had been so helpful to me over the years, to still assist me in writing my exams. Had he not warned me enough to study hard, not to be distracted, and remain a good girl?

The day I wrote my last paper of the final examinations, I felt relieved; a crushing load I had been carrying was suddenly lifted from my head. I was excited and happy that I had completed my undergraduate program. In a matter of days or a week, the results would be posted and I would append "B.Sc., Geography," the same qualification that made my father a secondary school principal, to my name. That evening I lowered my guard and, in the freedom of becoming a graduate and a young adult in a matter of days or a week, went to my boyfriend's room to pass the night. I was dazed with excitement of the day and went further with Ogaga than I had planned for the night. Exhausted, as I fell asleep, I saw a glimpse of my father's shadow disappearing. I started crying, but Ogaga did not know why I was crying. He might have thought of my losing my virginity that night. Only I knew why. He did not see what I saw. I felt I should have waited until the results of the exams were published. I was sad as I left the room at dawn.

A week after that sad day, the results were published. I made a Second Class Upper Division, the best grade in my class. I thanked my guardian and my father for making me a graduate. My father, I believed, had done me great. I would not see my father or, rather, he would not visit me again after that day to this day. Now I am a divorcee, only after three years of living with Ogaga. I am still jobless after graduation! And there is nobody to help me even after crying night and day that if my father were alive, my situation would have been much better. I wish I had waited only a week before I felt free enough to sleep in Ogaga's room.

CHAPTER TWO

* * *

The Old Man in
a State House

HIS LONG NAME EASILY GAVE him out as someone from a by-gone generation. Such names as his were no longer given. Ogbajiriemu. The strongman still eats! He has to in order to replenish his spent energy. Parents no longer wished their children the virtues of strength, physical or mystical, that the community once cherished because there were new realities of schooling and government work that they felt did not need the old virtues.

In place of sentence-long names of the olden days were contemporary word names that Ogbajiriemu's very young relatives now bore: Ese, Ufuoma, Efe, Igho, Ejiro, Tega, and many more. The new names strung together two syllables; not words strung together to form a sentence of a name. Ogbajiriemu, shortened to Ogbariemu by many, belonged to an era that had long passed with such names as Ochibejivwie, Omavuayiwhe, Omotejowho, and Oderhowho. Some of those names were parables meant to settle scores in their respective extended families. The old names made meaning then in the philosophy of life the people embraced. However meaningful such names might still be, Agbon people no longer had the patience to call such long names.

From birth he stood out, the main consideration for his parents naming him Ogbajiriemu. He was born big with open eyes and eating voraciously from his very first day. He sucked his mother's breasts as if he had been starving in the womb. He gulped water as if he came to a river for a new lease of life after parching and almost dying of thirst in a desert incarnation. He had fat toes and strong hands. His parents expected him to grow into a strongman to be feared and revered for his superhuman size. They also expected the mere invocation of his name to protect his relatives and neighbors. They hoped he would grow very big to become like the legendary Arhuaran of Benin, who, according to legends, circled the city three times with his over-sized right toe to create the three moats that protected the city from invaders. They wished their child would be the strongman who would protect them from all forms of hostility.

But Ogbajiriemu did not become a strongman. He grew big alright, but did not develop into the hulk of a giant that Arhuaran was fabled to be—not just being huge but also towering over every man in the kingdom of Benin. Agbon would not have another Arhuaran in Ogbajiriemu. His parents did not live long enough to be disappointed at the physical size of their adult son.

Ogbajiriemu would remain a peculiar man in his village. His parents were not diviners and so could not see the future beyond their living moments. They were ecstatic about their newborn child that came after five years of anxious waiting after marriage, and that was not all. That name summarized their joy. No longer would they doubt themselves or suspect others of wishing them to be childless. They did not know that they would abandon their child before long for another world, one after the other in quick succession. They did not know that their son would live a long life that was denied them, his parents. They did not know too that their son would be an ogre to future generations of the same village because of his longevity. Nor did they know that relatives would run away from their son and later be forced by economic circumstances to run back and embrace him in the same land of their ancestors. Of course, they knew that life was a mystery.

There was no way his parents' intuition or foresight could penetrate that far about their son's life—that he would possess such virtues that so many people would envy and wish for themselves. He would become what they could never foresee. He would, after a short and childless marriage, remain single in a society of goatish men always on heat. He would remain a mystery to future generations. It would have taken an adept diviner much reflection and sacrifice to crack the cowries of Ogbajiriemu's fate. Ominigbo, the renowned diviner, had not been put to death for long before his birth, but nobody connected the execution of the great Benin diviner to the birth of a simple Agbon baby boy.

For long the age gap between him and his fellow villagers was so wide that he was accused of the most horrendous of names: a wizard killing others to live long. He died by proxy, his critics said. He sacrificed others to pass through the year, others gossiped. He was a big tree whose branches were dying off, even as it grew taller and stronger. The accusations, for accusations they were, would not be done blatantly but indirectly done but meant for him to hear.

When relatives and villagers sought the answer to the mystery of others dying like chickens in an avian flu season and his living on like a terra cotta figure untouched by the adversities of time and seasons, they started to take drastic action. It was not the sort of action of stoning to death or assassinating whom they suspected thrived on the deaths of others. They just wanted to save their lives. They wanted to keep distant from him. They took a simple decision—if they could not overcome the evil spell he cast over others, he should be left alone. Singly and in groups of twos and threes at first, but later in droves, they abandoned him and moved to other villages and to Warri. Within three months, Ogbajiriemu became the sole inhabitant of a once teeming village.

Ogbajiriemu became an *akpobrisi* tree in the forest of a village. Only one *akpobrisi* stood in the forest and always surrounded by weeds and no other trees. The tree was said to be so strong mystically that its spirit destroyed any other tree around. As other trees kept distant from the *akpobrisi*, so did the inhabitants of the village keep distant from Ogbajiriemu. A great divide separated him from the rest of the world for a long time. Isolation made him reflect on so many things.

⁕ ⁕ ⁕

"Who knew that living by the roadside could be this strange?" Ogbajiriemu asked himself.

He was his own companion and not only talked to but also asked himself questions. He had now lived six decades in the house he had built as a young man of twenty-five. It was at that age that he, like his age-mates, had been considered mature enough to be a man and to marry.

Ogbajiriemu had chosen the piece of land by the goat-path then, soon to be taken over by the Public Works Department and made into a laterite-covered road that bicycles at first passed, and later widened for motor cars and lorries to ply. He and his friends used the *ifo* tradition of team work to build the house. Those he had helped to build theirs earlier were there to reciprocate, and it was such a thrilling experience for a house to rise in an open space within a few days. That house had transformed from a thatched mud house in the spirit of development into a cement-block house with corrugated iron sheets.

"Apart from this house," he mused, "there isn't really much else to show for the so many years of hard work. I still thank God for keeping me healthy and alive," he told himself.

Ogbajiriemu's house stood among abandoned houses in the village that once boasted of over sixty large families, but now accommodated only one old man. It was still called Okpokpo, the name the villagers had enthusiastically given to it when they moved from deeper inside the forest near the rest of the world, as they then put it. It was then a real "new" village. But the new had inevitably become old and Okpokpo now had only one resident. An uninhabited house deteriorated fast, and most of the abandoned homes were already collapsing. The seasonal downpours helped to bring down the mud houses among them. Kola nut, cocoa, and pepper fruit plants could still be found in the backyards of the fallen or falling homes. A little distance away, the *otie* cherry tree that used to bring young ones together to pick the delicious fruit stood wild amidst tall grasses. The cherry tree now only bore a few fruits and Ogbajiriemu did not need to sing the song that he had sung as a boy in a group running to be the first to be there at dawn to pick the sweet cherries. Most trees live longer than humans if they are not consumed by fire or cut down, the old man realized.

Once in a while, lost travelers stopped by Ogbajiriemu's house to ask him questions about what direction to take to someone who used to live in Okpokpo or to confirm the routes they were already taking but were not really sure of. Some travelers did not seem to be in a hurry and had time to exchange pleasantries and stories with Ogbajiriemu. From such tales and exchanges, the lone man of Okpokpo village knew about what was happening elsewhere: the scandals rocking near and distant communities and the development that was coming with the arrival of the foreigner, the so-called white man he had seen only once and from a distance. Also some of the travelers felt so relaxed as to cast jokes with him before continuing their journeys. At other times, he just pointed out the way to travelers that sought direction because the road forked into three directions just after the village. At night some travelers sang past the stretch of road by his house with its lamp visible from outside. Other travelers, either walking or riding bicycles on their way to known destinations, hummed incomprehensible songs in the dark. Ogbajiriemu could not understand why anyone traveling in the dark would consciously give himself out with a stream of songs.

The strongman still eats to replenish his strength! Ogbajir-iemu was a strongman who had overcome a multitude of vicis-situdes in his long life. He did not nurse any fear living alone; he feared neither fellow human beings nor wild animals and evil spirits. He was an offspring of not just a warrior but also of a hunter stock. Living alone or the dark did not scare him.

Knowing fellow human beings was a difficult task, he still believed at his age. However, now he understood the ways of humans. He had got used to human nature as he had done to the weather of his native place. Familiarity brought the experience, an advantage of age.

"Nobody wants to accept blame for his own mistakes. Nobody wants to accept his portion of life's unpleasantness, but everybody wants to claim sweet things," he told himself.

He knew from the bitter leaf that what was bitter could make sweeter what we wished for ourselves. He relished fresh fish bitter-leaf soup. Ogbajiriemu spent much of his lone life reflecting. His life had become a series of connected proverbs that he articulated whenever he observed simple things of life.

In a village abandoned to only one man, the signs of life were still there to see. Goats and chickens ranged freely—their respective bleating and clucking were music to the lone resident's ears. He had a small farm, a sort of garden, nearby. His bigger farm was some distance away.

∘ ∘ ∘

Ogbajiriemu was really not a strongman, the sort that tyran-nized his fellow villagers. His people had left the village on their own accord and without telling him why, though rumor publi-cized the fear of a man who lived on and on while all younger people were dying. Many placed his age at over one hundred years. He must have mystical or strange powers to live on like the feared *akpobrisi* tree surrounded by only grass and shrubs. No two of its kind were found in the same vicinity; only one flourished perhaps at the expense of other trees. Ogbajiriemu, to the former residents of Okpokpo, was a human *akpobrisi*, and it was dangerous living in the same village with him. It was even lethal being in his company, the rumor went. There was something diabolical in the *akpobrisi* tree that burned other plants nearby and left only grass and low shrubs!

Okpokpo villagers, with the exception of Ogbajiriemu, were dying from malaria, typhoid, running stomach, lockjaw, and a host of other ailments that killed without long symptoms. He was regarded as a strongman because the army of ailments that laid waste the rest of the village bypassed him and continued to decimate others, who were usually much younger than him. He became even stronger with age. He walked with the alacrity of a young man and his feet could barely touch the ground as he sprang in his fast walk. His body was taut and so while young men in their thirties were obese and dying, his body was compact.

How a name divined a person's life! Though not possessing the hulk of a giant, he carried the immunity of an exceptional strongman. He had never been slowed down by any sickness, never fallen ill, as far as those who had abandoned him believed was the case.

❖ ❖ ❖

"The eagle never misses its yearly return," Ogbajiriemu expressed his thought aloud as he saw the rare bird glide in from the northern horizon.

The *egodi* bird brought him a sense of nostalgia. It took him back to his childhood days when he and other children ran in the gliding manner of the highflying bird.

"The year passes on despite complaints!" he intoned.

Ogbajiriemu needed to talk, and he often talked. He talked to himself and at other times talked to the animals he kept.

He smiled when he saw the eagle appear from the horizon the way a parent received a traveled child returning home after a long absence. The migrant was not dead after all in the long absence but alive! What was absent was now present! The eagle was the symbol of constancy in a world full of sudden and slow changes. It kept its promise to the land to revisit yearly without ever failing. After each year's appearance of the eagle, Ogbajiriemu looked forward to the next appearance, another year of waiting that had always carried him through solitude to serenading the majestic bird.

"*Ugo, afo re!*" he praised the majesty of the white-feathered bird.

"When the time arrives, the year's ritual is performed," he said of the eagle.

Ogbajiriemu called some of his animals by name. The mother pig that had given birth to so many young ones, he called Poko. It was fat and had enough to eat on its own around. The he-goat that mounted all the female goats, he called Ariegha. He came by that name in the belief that it discriminated not on sex partners when on heat about the relationship and so committed taboos. He always turned away from looking at the he-goat's sexual escapades. Though he found its lifestyle repugnant, he had to keep it for the money it generated when it impregnated the female population. It was a money-making animal despite its dirty habits. He easily realized the contradiction he had to live with.

The chickens gave him little or no trouble. As long as they ranged freely, they sustained themselves. They went out at dawn and returned at sundown. The cocks among them crowed to forewarn of approaching dawn. They woke him to prepare for the day's task—farm work, fishing, or whatever he chose for the specific day. Once in a while, he treated himself with chicken pepper soup because he believed that one should enjoy out of one's bounties. He did the same with his pigs when he needed *banga* soup of pork with bitter leaf.

It was not only his cocks that woke him. He often heard from a distance away Christian bells and blacksmiths hammering very early in the morning. The sounds of drums of traditional worship came in late afternoon and continued till nightfall. Ogbajiriemu was also a fisherman. He fished in the Omoja, the Omwe, and the Uto, three rivers within a short distance of Okpokpo. He knew the habits of the different fresh-water fish around. Some could be caught with hooks; others could only be caught with cone nets that he knew how to weave from raffia branches and set at appropriate places and times. During the rainy season, when the streams and rivers were bloated, he took the road with a culvert to his fishing part of the Omoja River. There, at the culvert site, skipper and flying fish, instead of following the current, chose to fly over and came down on land across. They, of course, got stranded on land and were easy to pick. Ogbajiriemu wondered what reasoning informed the fish used to water to "jump" or "fly" over land into a place it was not sure of. He also reflected on the snake fish, the mudfish, and the electric fish, each very peculiar in its habits. To Ogbajiriemu, fish and animals were like human beings; each with its identity and idiosyncrasies.

One day in his fishing, Ogbajiriemu stood behind brushes in a wetland area to observe a kingfisher swoop down to catch fish at its will. It strutted and salivated on its catch. It made some grunting sounds to express its contentment. This went on for many minutes. Then crawled in a crocodile, first to the edge of the water and then onto land. There was abundant fish for both the kingfisher and the crocodile to sate whatever hunger was harrying them. Once the kingfisher saw the crocodile, it sprang into the air and flew away. Ogbajiriemu saw how some types of power surpass others.

Ogbajiriemu could not bring himself to hunt. He chose not to confront the wilds at night. He had heard stories of hunters witnessing animals transform into human beings and did not want to be shocked by such unexpected transformations as an antelope turning into a beautiful lady. He believed in dealing with the familiar. He set traps that he checked during the day. Once in a while he caught grass-cutter, deer, porcupine, and warthog, wild animals that were very tasteful and sold fast among his people.

He passed by a specific iroko tree that he named Uloho. He always paid homage to the huge tree whenever he was in its presence. The tree had a certain spiritual awe that held Ogbajiriemu spellbound.

"Uloho, king of trees, bring me prosperity and good health!" he intoned, like one addressing a god.

Then he nodded. A few times he threw coins at the foot of the tree. One pays homage to the king, he told himself. The iroko was king of the forest. That particular tree had been there from time immemorial and remained sturdy, unshaken by hurricanes and forest fires. There were times he felt drawn to the presence of that tree and sat under the canopy of its crown of green leaves for minutes. He had a spiritual experience of a certain calm that he could not explain to himself, but he felt great afterwards.

Could the forest tell its own story? The trees, animals, and birds must have stories to tell, as he had his own too, Ogbajiriemu mused. He talked to all of them when he had to. He invoked the beauties among trees, animals, birds, and fish. He saw how the bush community lived, each member minding its own business. Each creature's peace was also the others' peace. Their common foe was human beings that sought them for their pleasure. He wished he could live without hurting them, especially those in the bush that the Almighty kept away from being domesticated.

* * *

"Some days are more remarkable than others," Ogbajiriemu told himself.

For a man of his age, it took him a little long to come to that conclusion. His memory was now a huge house of many rooms, and he often moved from one to another. He enjoyed what each room offered in experience. So much variety that he went through in his regular life. Some of the rooms were pleasant—airy, comfortable, and full of delightful passion. He would like to remain in such rooms forever, but that was not possible. He had to move on, what he understood life to be. Other rooms were unpleasant—moldy, suffocating, and intolerably humid. Much as he would like to run out of such rooms, sometimes he was compelled by circumstances to remain there for some time. He savored the good experiences, even though he also cherished the bad ones.

"You learn from experience," he told himself.

He realized that it was from mistakes that he gained wisdom. Acts of folly and acts of wisdom feed on each other, he observed. He now knew that life was a learning experience. He did not suffer the illusion that one day he would be so wise, despite his age, that he would no longer make a mistake. As long as one lived, one would make mistakes and learn, he believed.

Ogbajiriemu, by virtue of his many years of living and the wisdom he had acquired, could tell the footmarks of a crab. He could tell the ruts of different animals in the bush from their make-ups and scents. He could tell by the smell of its urine the porcupine's rut. In the bush, his nose told him what animals had passed a spot and his eyes knew what animals had passed any part of the bush—the animals that tiptoed their way around and the ones that went gracefully in their haunts. He knew the false exit holes of the rabbit and the genuine ones.

"What is done properly brings no complaints," he told himself.

Ogbajiriemu had entered one of the many rooms in the huge mansion of memory. He had just remembered, when young, a woman wearing the mother-mask and performing so beautifully that, when discovered to be a female, nobody complained.

Rather, the female performer was lavished with praises for what men had claimed only they could do and often did clumsily. "It's a stunning phenomenon. Okurekpo women wear and dance the mask beautifully," the song went from mouth to mouth in the whole area. From that same masquerade performance also came the saying, "Who gives generously also receives lavishly in return." Okpara folks did not attend Kokori's masquerade festivities because they felt their neighbors were stingy; rather they went to Eku's performance to reciprocate with cash and other gifts their earlier generosity to them. Eku folks had made them proud at home; in return they would go and make them proud in their own home too.

"You reciprocate the generosity of others; that's life," Ogbajiriemu nodded, as he left that bright room for another room that did not possess the shine and glamour he had just experienced.

His first attendance of Ovughere came to his mind. It was a festival in honor of the tutelary god that protected Ovu people. The god's shrine stood in a roadside grove at the outskirts of town by the Omwe River. Bare-chested men in red skirts had their eyes circled with white chalk to show them as warriors. They clashed machetes in what appeared to be a mock battle. It remained a mock battle until the chief priest, Ejenavi, after slaying the ritual bull, got possessed by the god of war. Then he started attacking with his machete anybody he could get to in the crowd. He was believed to possess the *ekpo* charm that blunted the sharp edges of any metal wielded against him.

Spectators and initiates at Ovughere fell; blood splattered everywhere. Ogbajiriemu broke his leg and he still limped up till now from that incident of seventy something years ago. He could not bring himself to attend that festival again before it was discontinued after complaints from so many people to the District Officer at nearby Orerokpe. He lauded the discontinuation of the festival. Such senseless and violent practices needed to be done away with, he believed.

He closed the door to that room and stepped outside of the mansion of a thousand memories.

❖ ❖ ❖

Ogbajiriemu almost barged into Umukor, and both stepped backward in shocked response. Umukor was the only woman, really the only person, who had a relationship with Ogbajiriemu in his hermitage. She visited him, but he did not go to see her at Ogorivwo, the neighboring village some three miles away. Ogorivwo folks, especially the men, exchanged greetings with Ogbajiriemu when they met by chance in their fishing expeditions or while they passed him as they went to their farms. Even a few of those who had fled Okpokpo and did not move far but settled in Ogorivwo also greeted Ogbajiriemu when they passed him. Even his former neighbors did not want to be seen as openly hostile to him. Ogbajiriemu always smiled within at such people who had thought they were escaping and avoiding contact with him, but were fated to bump into him by chance from time to time.

Ogorivwo folks taunted Umukor as Ogbajiriemu's concubine and favorite. He gave the fish and animals he caught in nets and traps respectively to her to sell and return the proceeds to him. Usually, her prices for the fish and meat were affordable and she did not have to hawk them for too long. She had customers, who waited for her for the meat and fish. Ogbajiriemu's fish were live and not caught with poison, as many did with Gamalin 20 in lakes and large stretches of the river. He also did not use poisoned food as bait for the porcupine or deer he caught. Buyers knew what they were buying in any purchase from Umukor. It was Ogbajiriemu's catch. It tasted fresh and natural. His catch tasted the way fresh fish or meat was supposed to taste, the old complimented. The older men of Ogorivwo only ate his fish and meat or what they caught themselves. In addition to receiving an allowance for selling his fish and meat, Ogbajiriemu reserved for Umukor her choice meat and fish.

She was tall and plump, not a common combination in the women of Agbon who were usually thin and short. Besides, she was lively and looked very well-fed. To many in her Ogorivwo community, Umukor "bounced" and was the liveliest woman they could think of.

As for the assumption that she was Ogbajiriemu's concubine, Umukor felt it was futile explaining her relationship with the lone man of Okpokpo village or what remained of it. "They can't understand," she told herself. She did not waste her time and energy explaining the unbelievable.

And unbelievable their relationship really was. A fine woman, divorced for over two decades, visiting a single man who had all of Okpokpo Village to himself and not having an intimate relationship! Even if both of them stripped and ran naked after each other, there was nobody to see or stop them. If they opened the door of the house, they could still cavort in bed without fear of anybody barging into them.

And yet Ogbajiriemu and Umukor did not exploit the available opportunities before them. Ogorivwo adults could not imagine a relationship between the two of them without sex. That Ogbajiriemu did not visit Umukor mattered not in the public perception of their being lovers. They must be laughing together, the people said, meaning that they were very intimate friends.

◦ ◦ ◦

Ogbajiriemu was surprised that his quiet residence and haunt had suddenly turned noisy one late morning. He was surprised at the line of excited yellow helmet-wearing young men in white overalls dragging big hoses through the bush. These must be working for the strange-looking foreigner who supervised them. The old man observed the intruders cunningly without their noticing him. The intruders spoke English and talked excitedly. They had to be looking for something, which must be very precious to them, Ogbajiriemu believed. The bush now teemed with men. Once in a while there was a loud seismic boom, which shook the ground. This made the intruders shout in jubilation. They must have struck what they were looking for underground. But they did not leave; they continued dragging more hoses through the bush, and Ogbajiriemu continued to hear more of such booms that make the earth to tremble.

Through inquiry from Umukor, Ogbajiriemu would learn that the intruders were looking for a new type of oil used in driving cars and doing many other things. "What a strange world we live in!" he exclaimed. He was used to palm oil and palm kernel oil, but never knew that there was another type of oil underground that you had to tap from the earth's underbelly once you knew where pools of it lay.

Once the explorers found the new oil, more workers came into the place. There was a buzz in the air—something very precious had been found that would transform the place into a paradise. Plenty of money was going to be made.

Soon houses were being hastily constructed to accommodate some of the workers on a permanent basis there. Ogbajiriemu had thought they would collect whatever new type of oil there was underground and leave, but it appeared the intruders of his peace were there for the long haul. He learned that the oil was so plentiful that it could not be finished in a hundred years. He soon realized that the intruders and their find would outlive him in his own land. He had to think of ways to cope with the new situation. He had no problem with the strangers forcibly occupying his ancestral lands and those of his relatives who had moved away as long as they did not make life difficult for him. Gradually Ogbajiriemu would learn that, even in old age, there were many happenings or experiences that one could not predict.

It is a strange world, Ogbajiriemu had long learned. But the unexpected twist of events would make the world even stranger. There was a fresh influx of people to the land, the very land that his relatives and others had fled for safety's sake.

With the oil struck there and the bright prospects of so much wealth, the Federal Government suddenly got interested in the bush in which Ogbajiriemu and his people had lived for centuries. It was a military government that ruled with decrees and the gun and felt it could do whatever it wanted. It could rob people of their lands, as its soldiers had been robbing people of their property. Its praise-singers, who wanted to share in the new wealth, started to talk loud and write about the necessity for the Federal Military Government to take over all lands because of the mineral wealth involved.

And so in 1976 the military head of state enacted the Land Use Decree, which took over all lands in the country as belonging to the state. The government that seized power from elected representatives now seized the entire lands in the whole country. Of course, they would talk of compensations even as they robbed the populace of the area.

A new township started to be built near where many oil wells had been struck. Government surveyors, contractors, and engineers made money in the process of building an entire new town in the farmlands and bush of Ogbajiriemu's people. A satellite town also sprang up there of those servicing the oil workers. Make-shift restaurant owners, food sellers, young girls looking for men to satisfy to make money, and others got accommodation in ramshackle homes.

The township possessed all the manifestations of affluence. There were fine houses, cars, and other imported luxury goods. Apples from God-knows-where were hawked around for the residents to enjoy what their foreign company employers took for granted. The oil workers soon got a club where Nigerian and expatriate workers danced and struck sex deals.

* * *

People who had flooded to the city or migrated to nearby villages started to return to sell their abandoned lands and farmlands. They backdated agreements of the lands they now sold out to pre-1976 in court affidavits. With so much money involved, there were many land disputes that only the very old person around was asked to testify to the ownership of pieces of land. Every party disputing land courted Ogbajiriemu's favor to testify to the ownership of the land in question. A magistrate court was set up in a trailer house near Ogbajiriemu's home to adjudicate on land disputes.

"Ogbajiriemu is my grandfather's cousin and friend and knew all our family lands," one side would testify.

"Ogbajiriemu is our relative and knows this is our land," another side would counter.

The winning side would later embrace Ogbajiriemu in a show of family solidarity.

After so many years of his exclusion from society, he could not catch up with the language the younger ones spoke; on their part, the younger ones saw him speaking an antiquated language and could only understand snatches of it.

❖ ❖ ❖

The old man could hardly breathe but said he would die in his own house. He would not accept the generous offers of Bell Oil Company to leave his house for a modern one that would be built and furnished for him. Nor would he accept a hefty sum of money he could not imagine how to spend during the rest of his life.

"When my relatives fled, I remained here and will not leave now. I have lived here all my life. I built this house to live in and not to abandon it. A man does not abandon his home no matter what. He defends his home. I will live and die in this house that I built with the help of my age-mates who are now all gone beyond. I don't know what it feels like living there, but I am not in a hurry to join them. I am already late anyway and I will join them when the Almighty One chooses. Everyone has his turn of doing things. It has not been my turn to die yet and I will accept when my turn comes.

That the world I once knew is now gone is no reason for me to abandon my home. One world goes, another world comes, and the world is ever changing. It is the world that one is stuck with that one lives. I have seen the good and now must endure the bad of my world here. I have lived with people and have been living alone for so many years.

A man has to stand up to his rights and my house is my house, no matter what foreigners and government say about my inherited land. Government and the foreigners have no ancestors here; they have not buried their forefathers and mothers here to claim it as theirs. The land is mine and my people's even though they had abandoned their portions. They fled but they are still my people and we own the land. A land's rightful owner does not change. It can be given out voluntarily. It can be sold to others. But the land's true owners are always only one. The government can send papers which I can't read that it has taken over the land, but it is wrong to claim what is not its own. Government should not be a robber. I will not give in to any robber. I will die protecting my own property from being taken away."

He began reflecting on the environment when he was young—the lush evergreens, the pure streams with plenty of fish, the fertile lands and abundant crops, and the communal world he knew now gone. He realized that as he was no longer his old self, so had the land also changed. The more he remembered what used to be, the more adamant he became and resolved to remain where he had always lived.

There was not much Bell Oil Company or the Federal Military Government could do about a stubborn old man who refused to quit his land despite such a staggering offer. He was a big obstruction to the exploitation of oil since his house stood atop a sea of oil. Evicting him could result in a publicity nightmare. And what if, in the process of evicting him, he resisted and died? Nothing could be more scandalous than a big multinational company and a military government killing an old man to make money. They would wait. He might not live for too long again, they surmised. And so, by virtue of the State owning all lands in the country, Ogbajiriemu's house was no longer just his own property but a State house.

CHAPTER THREE

❖ ❖ ❖

The Cherry Tree Palaver

"*OTIE MR'OVWATA, K'OSHE-EE*," the song went.
When the cherry tree sees its favorite, it showers its fruits lavishly on the person. The singers addressed their song to the god of songs and music that inspired them. The ripe cherry fruit, whose juice and flesh had an inimitable flavor and were so delectable, was compared to the most beautiful of songs that could be composed or sung.

Nobody knew who had planted the cherry fruit trees that grew outside the residential parts of many villages. None of the very old, including Pa Iniovo, knew the tree when it was young and not yet producing the tasty fruits that old and young, men and women, so cherished. Everybody grew up to see the fruiting tree in that part of Unoh village. That tree must have grown before anybody started to live there. Or it was planted by the founders of the ageless village. So the cherry tree of Unoh village, famous for its large, bell-like, and uniquely tasty fruits, had been there from the beginning of time. If nobody knew its age, then it was the Supreme Being who planted it, many people believed.

Alone, at the northern end of the village, a brisk walk away and in a bushy area, stood the cherry fruit tree. While a marked but seldom cleared path took one to the tree, its grounds and surroundings were left alone. Perhaps the people believed that ripe fruits should fall on grass-covered soil to prevent them from breaking upon impact with the ground. Those who garnered the fallen fruits beat the path of grass and weeds with their feet. It was a frequented place during the fruiting season and no child of the village would grow up to be a man or a woman without having waited for the fruits to fall and then racing with age-mates to pick them.

"Who rises early and races fastest picks the ripest cherry fruits," the saying also went.

Nobody went to pick fallen fruits at night. Everybody waited for early dawn when children came to a meeting point and from there the cluster sprang out to outrun each other and get to the tree to pick the fruits that had come down in showers overnight. Some of the ripest ones that had fallen got covered by weeds or dry leaves. After picking the fragrantly visible fruits, the children would comb for others half buried in the soft moist soil. It was fun for the children, searching around for hidden fruits that only keen eyes could find.

"Night replenishes the day's depletion," the old said, refer-ring to the cherry fruit tree and the abundance of fruits to be picked at dawn.

The tree grew very tall before spreading branches in all directions. Its leaves remained deep green every season, wet or dry. Nobody touched it with a cutlass or axe. One could cut other trees, use their barks or roots for medicinal purposes, but not of the cherry fruit tree that was everybody's favorite. Other trees could be cut down for furniture or firewood, but not the otie tree. Its proverbial generosity to all protected it from being cut. Nobody guarded it, but it stood safe from poachers.

No child used a stick or club to force down the fruits. Nor did any child shake the fruiting tree for the fruits to fall down, since it was too massive to shake. The children saw ripe and un-ripe fruits weighing down the tree branches high up, but none climbed the tree to pluck the ripe ones. It was unheard of to pluck the fruit from the tree's stems. One waited for the fruits to ripen and fall. When it was windy or stormy, the otie tree showered fruits for those around. As for the fruits, once tasted one would always come for more. There was also the saying that the tree's favorite always arrived at the time the fruits would be falling down. *Otie mr'ovwata ko she-e.* The tree was the people's example of fate—namely that God gave to those that pleased Him. The people's God or divine spirit lived in the *otie* tree.

Many very old people believed that benevolent spirits gathered there at night to have a parley and looked for ways to bless good people and to punish bad ones in the community. There, too, played spirits of beautiful and good children who wanted to come to life by entering the wombs of the women they loved. The girls were aware of this, having been told by their mothers who also had been told by their mothers—to go and pick *otie* fruits; there the spirit children would see them and later choose them as their future mothers. It was the young girls' protection, as future adult women, against barrenness and childlessness, two of the worst conditions that a woman could be cursed with among them. The cherry fruit tree blessed those who came to pick its ripe fruits.

Many young ones made their first money from hawking the fruits on a platter. Some women took the fruits to the market to sell. The *otie* fruit sold fast because the buyers associated so many good things with it. It made children sharp and attentive, more so later when they went to school. It made the women fertile and reduced their pregnancy problems. It made the men folks vigorous. The *otie* fruit was a favorite of everybody, young and old, women and men. Every day in its fruiting season came those who cherished the fruit or wanted to be associated with its blessings.

Recently, many in Unoh village converted from traditional religious worship into the Church of the New Dawn, a Pentecostal brand of Christianity. They were very fervent in their belief in Jehovah, the God they carried in their hearts and heads like a talisman around. They invoked Jehovah, especially his son Jesus Christ, and the Bible to solve any problems that confronted them. They did not only go to church on Sundays but also had Bible classes on Wednesdays and Fridays and all-night vigil every Friday. Many returned from their farms early to attend church activities. The adherents of the faith, who saw demonic hands in every difficulty or problem they encountered, believed that their pastor, Emmanuel, cast out demons from their lives.

Pastor Emmanuel had come to Unoh village from Warri, where he had lost a majority of the members of his small congregation to another pastor on the same street. A tall and thin man in his late forties, he prayed and reflected for several weeks and took the drastic action of abandoning the remaining ten or so members of his congregation to start afresh in a new location. He had started to grow a beard before he arrived at Unoh village. His voice had always been vibrant, as if from a more muscular frame, and he arrived with the intention of putting in his best in the service of God, as he saw his mission among welcoming villagers who saw him as the one who would deliver them from poverty, death, and evil forces they felt were rampant among them.

Pastor Emmanuel prayed for financial breakthrough for members of his congregation in the prevailing economic hardship that seemed to have chronically afflicted them.

"Jehovah will turn your lives around," he thundered, his hands outstretched.

The congregation rose from the wooden benches on which they sat.

"Amen," they echoed back.

"Jesus will destroy the demons preventing you from prospering," Pastor Emmanuel shouted forcefully.

"Amen."

"Praise the Lord!"

"Alleluia!"

As the prayer reached a crescendo, many in the congregation shook their hands and heads, starting to be possessed by the power of the pastor's voice. Then all started dancing gracefully to the percussive rhythm of the choir that started a familiar song. Pastor Emmanuel had specially asked that drums be beaten in the church service so that the Holy Spirit would enter the congregation at special moments. None of his Unoh village congregation knew that the drumming in the other church that drew most of his church members had informed his realization that drums were a good means of keeping the service lively.

As life became harder for the people, a majority of whom had joined the Church of the New Dawn to prosper, Pastor Emmanuel's prayers against demonic forces became more strident. Standing before the lectern, beside a high table that formed the altar, he realized that his words had to be powerful to have the desired results.

"We have to destroy the evil forces that hold us down," he prayed.

"Thank the Lord!" they chorused back.

"We cast into hellfire the demons dragging us into poverty," he intoned.

Soon the converts started to look for not only the demons that held them down but also ways to destroy them forever. People were getting sick—too many malaria and typhoid patients. Men and women suffered from hernia and many went to Eku Baptist Hospital and did not return. Women had miscarriages. Malformed babies were being born in large numbers. Others were having the "urinating disease" and some had become blind; others had their feet amputated. Once in a while a huge and healthy-looking important member of the church collapsed and died.

"What is going on?" the fervent believers in the Church of the New Dawn asked themselves.

They searched their lives and surroundings for the causes of their economic problems, diseases, and death. Soon, Amakashe, the most outspoken of the converts, pointed at the huge cherry tree as the meeting place of witches that wreaked havoc on the village population.

"It's the *otie* tree that causes our problems," he announced.

Amakashe was a smallish but fierce-looking man. He had bulging eyes that would scare children seeing him for the first time. He walked with a limp. After converting, Amakashe had, in an open-air service, testified that he had been a native doctor but had, on the day of his being born again, gathered his paraphernalia and tools and set them ablaze. As part of the testimony, he told the pastor and others in the church that he had broken his pact with Satan and was now God's child. Pastor Emmanuel respected and feared him and sought his counsel on how to further convert the few diehard traditionalists left in the village and around. Those diehards were allies of Satan causing daunting problems for the others, he believed.

Pastor Emmanuel took the cue from Amakashe, whom he trusted as knowing about demonic powers in the community on which his Church of the New Dawn thrived.

"We must destroy the tree; that is the origin of our problems," he promulgated.

While many shifted uneasily on their seats, unsure of what Pastor Emmanuel meant, a few others like Amakashe and Agogo took it as an order to mow down the *otie* fruit tree.

Nobody owned the otie fruit tree, though the Unoh village community assumed it owned it. After all, unlike other fruit trees such as the orange, mango, and pawpaw, the cherry tree was in nobody's compound to be claimed as individually or family-owned. It grew in the community-owned land that was part of the village.

❈ ❈ ❈

The argument between Pa Atubi, one of the converts, and his eldest son, Efe, a Senior Lecturer of Botany at the University of Benin, testified to the crisis in the community and how bad things had become. When Dr. Efe Atubi visited home, he had in mind walking round to meet and greet his extended family members and his age-mates who remained behind to farm rather than go to school like he did. He was brilliant and had his Ph.D. at the relatively young age of thirty.

Pa Atubi was proud that his son he had spent his life's earnings to send to school built him the most modern house in the village. It was a four-bedroom bungalow roofed with zinc. Since Efe's mother's death, Pa Atubi had remained unmarried and did not listen to the calls of fellow villagers to take a young wife at his age. The parlor of his house was large and sat over a dozen cushioned chairs. He had his favorite cane chair, which he positioned specially only for himself to watch the television his son had also bought for him.

He was sitting in his cane chair when his son came in to greet him.

"How is the University?" Pa Atubi asked his son.

"Fine! Only we are on strike again," he told his father.

"You university teachers are more interested in going on strike to raise your salaries than teaching your students," he said.

"It's not so, Pa. We are doing our best. Do you know a junior civil servant earns more than I, a Senior Lecturer, do?" Efe asked.

"Let me talk about what I know," Pa Atubi continued, knowing the passion with which his son always talked about the salaries of university teachers.

He paused for a moment to look at his son in the face.

"Efe, there is a big problem here. We are thinking of cutting down the *otie* tree," he began.

"God forbid such a bad thing!" Efe interrupted. "No, no, no! Nobody should do such an abominable thing," the academic said.

"We are bent on cutting it down because it has become the coven of witches around," Pa Atubi explained.

"What do you mean by that?" Efe asked.

"Witches meet there and cause too many problems in the village. The *otie* fruit tree has become their assembly ground in plotting evil for people," the father further explained.

"What of the many good things that the tree and its fruits do that you used to preach to me about? How can a tree that is so important to all of us and makes the village more habitable be the cause of its problems?" he asked.

"University education has robbed you of your senses," Pa Atubi said.

"No, being born again has changed you, Pa," the son told his father.

Dr. Efe Atubi felt he had to thread carefully on this controversy that had gripped his community. Telling the people about how important the otie tree was to their culture would not solve the problem. He had seen how that argument had not worked to persuade his own father against cutting the tree down. He would talk to them about it from the environmental aspect.

Very few people felt Efe knew what was happening and that he was meddling into what he did not know about, and so did not want to listen to him. He talked to a group of four men, his father's fellow Christians. They had come to discuss some of their church matters with Pa Atubi.

"If you destroy the environment, the damaged environment will hurt you too," he reasoned.

"Which do you prefer to be eliminated from among us, poverty and disease or the *otie* fruit plant?" Amakashe asked him.

"The tree brings health in so many ways to us. Like every other tree around, its existence makes us live better lives. More so the *otie* fruit tree has been with us from time immemorial and our lives are linked to it," he further explained.

"Ehe—e! Its being linked to our lives is causing too many problems in our lives, even taking our lives. That is why we should destroy it," Amakashe jumped in.

"The cherry tree cannot be the demon snuffing lives out of our people," the academic told his audience that had grown. His father and three other men had joined the original four men to listen to him.

"It is what we eat and drink that cause most of our ailments," he continued.

"Education is making you lose your mind," Amakashe said.

"Did you say what we have been eating and drinking cause our problems? Do they also cause our poverty?" Agogo asked.

"We eat bad foods and drink too much. We need to change what we eat—not just yam, garri, rice, oil soup, and the rest of them," he tried to explain to them.

"He is surely out of his mind; if not how dare he describe what our ancestors ate and lived healthily till a very ripe age now cause us problems," Amakashe remarked.

"We are really not eating the same foods and taking the same drinks," Dr. Efe contended.

"How? Are the crops we grow not the same as before? Is the *amreka* gin not the same *amreka* gin that gave energy and vitality to our ancestors?" Amakashe asked in a rather derogatory tone.

"You should know that things have changed," Dr. Atubi said, in response to Amakashe. "Do we eat the water leaves, mushrooms, beans, and the so many fruits that our people used to eat?" he asked.

"Are you telling me that mushrooms and water leaves are better than rice and garri?" Amakkashe asked back.

"Of course, vegetables and fruits are better than the starchy foods that our people now only take," Dr. Atubi explained.

There was silence as if to digest what the university senior lecturer had said.

"And you are blaming our *amreka* gin too on our poverty and deaths too?" Agogo asked.

"Is *amreka* still distilled from palm wine as it used to? No, it is now brewed from dangerous chemicals," he said, mocking the lack of observation of those arguing with him.

The exchange had become noisy and it was getting dark and it soon dawned on Dr. Atubi and the others that none would be able to persuade the other, and so they dispersed.

Dr. Efe Atubi left for his University with a heavy heart and the folks in the village had to deal with the problem before them.

For weeks the Pentecostal converts discussed how best to destroy the demon of a tree. Some wanted kerosene or petrol to be doused around it and setting it on fire. Amakashe suggested that tires be placed on the tree, fuel poured into the tires, and then ignited. However, he did not explain how one could wear a tire over a tree of the cherry tree's size. In the end, the converts decided to cut it down with an axe or a machete. And the deed should be done at night when the witches would be meeting there.

"We have to confront them so that they know that the blood of Christ protects us from all their demonic ways," Pastor Emmanuel explained at the Sunday service.

"Surely, the blood of Christ protects God's children," the congregation chorused.

Amakashe was one of the many men who took on the task of cutting down the ageless cherry fruit tree about midnight. At a point in the cutting down of the cherry fruit tree, the converts passed the axe or cutlass, whichever tool each chose to use, from one hand to another to show that each of them was participating in the destruction of the tree's resident demon. It was the combined effort of the members of the Church of the New Dawn that destroyed the *otie* tree, the demon they saw as destroying their lives. The deed was done in three hours amidst hysteric chants of "Die, demon die!"

At the crashing of the tree, Amakashe and Agogo raised another song, "God's power conquers Satan's power," to which they sang and danced deliriously for a half hour. It was like the celebration of an epic victory that involved songs, prayers, and dance. The "born-again" converts had demolished the cherry tree; in their minds they had conquered Satan.

* * ◆

By the time that Dr. Efe Atubi visited home two months later, the story of the destroyed "demonic" *otie* fruit tree was on everybody's mouth. Efe's father narrated to him what had happened. In the verandah where he had fixed three cane arm-chairs, he sat in one and his son in another. It was a cool evening, after a late afternoon downpour.

"We couldn't help but destroy the tree," he began. "It took more than thirty hefty men to hack it down in three hours and it took over twenty more men another two hours to cut the trunk into pieces that were set on fire in the open field because nobody would accept to cook with that type of demonic wood."

Efe imagined the orange blaze of the pieces of wood burning at the dawn hour. However, he suddenly felt cold. It was as if he had lost a limb or some other important part of his own body, the way his village had lost the cherry tree.

"The tree was so tough that those cutting it down felt as if a hand was holding them back to slow them from performing the task before them. It was as hard as stone. That tree was more than an ordinary tree. The spirit in it was too strong," and he paused to look at his son's face.

Efe squeezed his face, pained by the savagery meted on the *otie* fruit tree. He had a sudden headache.

"To show you there was something demonic about the tree, the sap was red. Have you ever seen a tree with human blood?" Pa Atubi asked.

Efe did not respond. He bit his lips. He knew that any tree as old as the *otie* would be a daunting task to hew down with an axe or cutlass by whatever number of men, one at a time. With its age, it had the toughness gained from centuries of existence. Also, with its age, the tree's sap should turn pink like the juice of its fruits. He realized that it was the pink color that his father said was red like human blood. How could the villagers know red at night? But what use telling his father that what he had described was all wrong? After all, he reflected, the damage had been done. He realized that there were actions whose negative consequences could not be reversed. The *otie* tree was gone forever.

"You have caused more problems for the people than tried to solve the existing ones," Efe later began. "Trees, animals, birds, and we human beings are all inter-dependent and form a harmony in coexistence. By destroying the *otie* fruit tree, you have destroyed that harmony. The death of one is the death of others, however slowly the subsequent deaths might come," he concluded.

It took him another one year, longer than normal, to visit the village again. He had been promoted to a Professor. He was summoned home because his father was sick. The problems of the people had not diminished but, in fact, redoubled; his father confessed to him before he died. Amakashe had been stricken with a stroke and had become paralyzed and very frail. Two of the most zealous in the cutting down of the cherry fruit tree had died after a brief illness. Agogo also had been crippled by a strange disease.

The pastor had noticed the Sunday collection dwindling at an alarming rate. This place was cursed, he told himself. Why could his congregation not be rich and make God happy by giving record offerings. He soon fled Unoh village after complaining publicly of nightmares he could not dispel with deliverance services.

Efe knew that the cherry fruit tree palaver had not resolved his people's problems.

"How will witches not be many and doing havoc among a people who continue to eat starch, garri, yams, palm oil and its soup, coconut, and other unhealthy foods? Have they stopped taking *amreka*, now brewed from toxic chemicals instead of from palm wine?" he asked himself.

He had told his people this before but they did not believe him. Thinking of the victim *otie* fruit tree, he shook his head.

A new pastor had come from Warri to quickly take over Pastor Emmanuel's place. It was as if it was a smooth succession arrangement in which no disruption took place in the activities of the church. Everything fell into place. All the village "born again" Christians held to their positions and their views. The Pentecostal population continued to increase without changing their lifestyles and growing increasingly fervent about their faith. And, of course, getting more impoverished and dying at an alarming rate! Efe did not know what the next scapegoat would be.

CHAPTER FOUR

Birthing Generations

U MUTOR HAD JUST ARRIVED IN Charlotte, North Carolina, from Okpara in Nigeria to take care of her daughter, who had delivered through a caesarian section procedure. It was also a premature birth, and both nursing mother and baby were in a bad state of health. Hence Umutor was driven from the airport straight to Carolinas Medical Center, where Ufuoma and her baby were both recovering. She had asked to be taken directly to where her daughter and grandchild were, and her son-in-law had complied.

"Osonobrughwe, take care of my daughter and grand-child," Umutor had prayed throughout her long plane journey.

On the way to the hospital, she continued invoking her ancestors to keep Ufuoma and the baby healthy and strong. As far as she knew, no Isaba family mother had met any mishap at delivery. She also knew of no Isaba daughter or grandchild who had died from delivery complications.

"Let it not happen to me. Let it not happen that an Isaba daughter had problems with delivery. Let it not happen that an Isaba baby did not survive infancy," she prayed.

"Once an Isaba, always an Isaba! And as at home in Okpara, so also abroad!" she chanted to her ancestors, whose spirits she believed would surely hear and heed her prayers wherever she was.

· · ·

Umutor recollected clearly what had happened before she conceived her first child, a son, now working with the National Petroleum Company in Port Harcourt. How generations of women differ, she reflected.

She had married when she was barely sixteen, which was rather normal in her time. She looked physically more mature than her age because she appeared already marriageable, according to her parents. She expected that, once married, she would conceive in a matter of months.

"One child at a time and the home soon fills up," her elders had prayed for her.

She had expected to have a full house if the Supreme One would be generous to her. She loved babies and wanted boys and girls to fill her home. She wanted a noisy home, and that meant many children. That would give her immense happiness and fulfillment, she had hoped.

She had been very naïve for her age. She had not started menstruating when she was escorted as a young bride to her husband's house. Her mother, who knew this situation, had not been worried. She had waited till a few days before her daughter would be escorted to her husband before addressing the issue. The mother called her daughter in, sat her on the bed facing her and began to counsel her about marriage. She knew Umutor would not ask questions, but told her that she would need to start menstruating before she could be pregnant.

"It happens many times. Some women start early, others late," she told Umutor.

To their relief, Umutor began menstruating three months after getting to her husband's home. Once she started menstruating, she expected the floodgate of conception to open.

Six months passed. Then nine months, and not too long later a year passed. She expected the exhibit of her lovemaking to show to the world so that her parents and others would congratulate her. She wanted to show her big tummy as a sign that her husband was taking good care of her. She wanted to be petted by her husband because she had heard that men petted their pregnant wives. She just wanted that special experience of conception; after all, that would make her more of a real married woman.

However, every month her monthly cycle brought her menstruation and frustration. By the eighteenth month, her menstrual period started to irritate her. It had turned to an unwanted guest. It was not welcome. She would prefer not to see it. Two years passed. Three years passed and there was no evidence that she would miss her period and start the nine-month mountain climb that would result in a baby's cry.

The fourth year of her marriage had coincided with the Elohor Masquerade performance, when the goddess of fertility was believed to bless women who had been married and had not conceived. The masqueraders were covered but were known to be men. Women who wanted the blessings of the gods and ancestors bought white dresses to wear during the four-day masquerade performance.

Umutor bought white calico that was sewn into the special three-piece dress for the occasion. She looked up to the festival with great expectations. She realized that would be the chance for her to conceive, if she performed her role well during the festival. She did not doubt the power of her husband to impregnate her. She would seize the opportunity of the festival to awaken her womb to its responsibilities.

She remembered when at the village square the chief masquerade, who wore the mother mask, came to her in the line of young women like her seeking conception.

"You are young and beautiful. Spirit children that will become babies in our world will vie to come to you to deliver," the masquerade had prayed.

"*Ise-e*," she had intoned.

"I say they will compete to enter your womb," he again told her.

"*Ise-e*," she again intoned.

"When next I visit, I want you to boast of the many children you have," the chief masquerader continued.

"*Ise-e*," Umutor responded.

The chief masquerader then threw white chalk powder at her. He also placed on her outstretched right palm chalk powder, some of which Umutor licked, and the rest she rubbed over her stomach. That, she believed, would make her womb fertile.

Umutor was so invigorated by the activities of the Elohor Masquerade festival that she became more vivacious than ever. She felt different—spritely and yet calm. She could feel sensations in her body and mind as she had never experienced. She was confident that her life would change for the better because she believed in the efficacy of the prayers of the mother mask of Elohor.

True to her belief in the efficacy of the prayers of the masquerade, Umutor conceived within six months and got her first child, a boy, in her fifth year of marriage. Two girls followed in quick succession and, by the next masquerade dance, she was appreciative of the prayers but then had no need to wear the white dress again. She was already thrice a nursing mother. She presented gifts of cigarettes, *sosorobia* perfume, and money to the masqueraders. Ufuoma came last, her fifth child.

* * *

Now in Charlotte in the summer and on her way to the hospital, Umutor tried to string together her conversation with her daughter the past three years.

Ufuoma did not marry early, as her mother had done. She had taken her studies seriously and had received her B.Sc. degree in Nursing from the University of Ibadan. After graduation, she had worked at the Central Hospital in Warri for several years.

She was thirty-seven when she married Efetobore, a Kokori man, who had gone to the United States for over fifteen years, first to study and then to work. He had several buildings in Warri and appeared to be doing well. At forty-two, many wondered why a prosperous man like him would wait for so long before marrying. But he was attractive in many ways to Ufuoma, who had no hesitation in agreeing to marry him.

"You must count yourself lucky when you know that nurses are well paid in America," her nurse friends at the Central Hospital, Warri, had told her.

She met the same encouragement at home. Visiting her mother in Enemejuwa Street, her mother sat her down in her sparsely furnished sitting room of three cushioned chairs and a center table. Ufuoma knew her mother was excited and had something important to tell her.

"Your waiting is worth it," Umutor told her, happy that she was having a son-in-law in America.

"One day I will be there too, after you have gone there," she again told Ufuoma.

"You should come to assist me take care of my first baby at least. You'll teach me the experience of nursing a baby," Ufuoma had told her.

"That is every mother's dream, taking care of her grandchildren. I will be more than ready to do that," she had assured Ufuoma.

After the marriage, Ufuoma joined Efetobore in the United States. She was happy to be married and to be in America; her husband was happy to be married to a home girl, as he described Ufuoma, rather than to an *akata*, an African-American woman, who would not understand his culture as he too would not understand her ways of a married life. The new couple hoped to start a family immediately, since both had passed the normal age for marriage among their people.

Six months passed. Ufuoma started to receive frequent phone calls from her mother and father, in Nigeria.

"How are you? When are we having our grandchild through you?"

"Whenever it comes," she answered.

"We are eagerly waiting," the mother would add.

Two years passed without the anticipated conception.

"What are both of you waiting for?" Umutor queried Ufuoma.

"What do you want me to do?" she asked back.

"Is he well?" the mother also asked.

"He does everything a man should do," she explained, a little embarrassed, but feeling she needed to make clear to her mother that her husband was neither impotent nor sick in any way she could tell.

The third year passed. Ufuoma was already doing well as a nurse at Carolinas Medical Center, where she got employment almost as soon as she got her work permit.

"Do you want me to see a grandchild from you or what?" the mother asked on the phone.

"God's time is the best," she replied.

"Both of you should do something. No Isaba woman marries without having children. Do something!" Umutor told her as an order.

"You are not getting younger anymore. As the day advances, the palm juice becomes scanty."

These statements reminded Ufuoma that not only her biological clock but also her husband's were ticking away and time was not on their side. As a nurse, she read and knew how it got more difficult for an aging couple to get a baby and, sometimes if they got, their child could be retarded in one way or another. For her man, she could tell that he was not as strong as he used to be. Of course, his sperm count should be much lower now than it used to be. As for herself, she was getting scared of suddenly starting her menopause without conceiving. That should not be allowed to happen, she told herself. It would be taboo for her to menopause without a single pregnancy.

Ufuoma became anxious at the end of her cycle. Would there be a break in the cycle or the same disappointing routine would continue? She asked herself.

The man was also getting anxious. He did not express it, but he was worried over the situation of being married for five years and no child yet to show for the married life. His wife had not conceived. There was not even a miscarriage. Could any of them be the cause? He asked himself many questions that he did not want to answer personally.

The couple did not talk to each other about the situation for a long time, as if keeping quiet would remove the problem that gnawed at their minds all the time. Later they went for counseling. That was after Ufuoma watched a program on television about couples having sexual or other problems discussing such with a registered professional third party.

Pam King, an experienced marriage and fertility counselor, had her office in the State Social Work Department Building. Always dressed in her senior nurse white uniform, she was very affable. She made her office as homely as possible. She and her two visitors sat round a table set to project an air of confidentiality.

"How long have you been married?"

"More than four years!"

"Have you had any children, pregnancies, or abortions?
"None!"

"Is it by choice or you can't help it?

"Certainly not by choice," Efetobore answered.

"Have you considered adopting a child or having your own through new medical procedures?" the counselor asked.

"Not till now," Ufuoma answered for both of them.

It was then that Ufuoma and Efetobore started thinking seriously about either adopting a child or getting one through in vitro fertilization. "I will like to have my own baby from our blood rather than adopt," Ufuoma told her husband.

She wanted to prove that she was fertile and capable of conceiving through whatever method possible.

"I don't mind if we have a child by adoption or any medical procedure," the man said.

"I prefer in vitro fertilization. Let the doctors help us to have a baby from our own genes," she told him before the counselor, who watched the couple discuss the choices before them.

He knew she was serious about giving birth herself rather than having a child through adoption. She rarely argued over things this way and he knew that conceiving and delivering meant much to her.

"Let's go for it," Efetobore told his wife.

"That's fine with me," she responded.

The counselor felt her work had been made easy for her. She gave the couple pamphlets on in vitro fertilization to read and then to call the clinic of their choice.

In three months they put together the huge sum of thirty thousand dollars charged for the procedure. Their health insurance did not cover that, they learned from inquiry. Once they paid the sum, they went to The Child Production Clinic in Almond Street, where they were examined. Later they were coached on how to get the man's sperm, which would then be saved and implanted by the doctor into the woman's ovary at the appropriate time in her ovulating cycle. That was how Ufuoma got pregnant the fifth year of her marriage, when already forty-two.

The conception gave her problems, not just because it was a first but because her husband's seeds planted in her womb could not fully acclimatize to it. She had looked to pregnancy to bring her happiness and fulfillment, but it gave her worries throughout. There was no month she did not have a pregnancy-related sickness. She prayed for the day she would deliver and be free of the pregnancy.

It was in the seventh month that, to save the baby and the mother, a caesarian section was performed. Ufuoma's mother was hastily brought in to save the situation because there was not only nobody to take care of the newly delivered mother with Efetobore working to pay insurance debts and other bills but also no milk in the nursing mother's breasts.

* * *

The mother arrived at the hospital with trepidation and joy that her daughter had at last delivered. Isaba would make sure that both nursing mother and baby were fine, she assured herself. If Ufuoma could be pregnant—and she was not told how it came about—she and her baby would be fine. The ancestors were keeping guard of them, Umutor believed.

Umutor looked at her daughter's neat hospital room as soon as she settled down; it was more like a hotel room than a hospital room, she reflected. But this was not the time to compare America and her Nigeria. There was an emergency at hand that she felt she had to deal with.

"Do they sell palm wine in this town?" Umutor asked Efetobore.

"Yes," he answered.

"Go and buy some bottles or calabashes for Ufuoma to drink," she ordered.

"I won't drink it," Ufuoma said.

"It will cure your lack of breast milk," Umutor explained.

"Unfortunately, my doctor will not allow me to drink it. I have diabetes resulting from the pregnancy. Mom, the pregnancy had been a big problem," she explained.

"Don't worry. Go and buy the palm wine so that I can drink it," Umutor explained.

Umutor drank and drank palm wine like water. She emptied bottle after bottle. She was not drunk. By the third day her breasts had milk and she started to breast-feed the premature baby.

Three weeks later, to the astonishment of the doctors, Ufuoma, and Efetobore, the child was strong enough for mother and child to be discharged from the hospital. For Umutor who knew the ancestors had specially given her the breast milk to nurture her granddaughter to good health, her real babysitting for her daughter began. Her being in America also really began.

CHAPTER FIVE

❖ ❖ ❖

Sharing Love

I EXPERIENCED THE LONGEST NIGHT of my life so far the day that Kena came ready for me. It was a sleep-free night that brought me more than I had wished for, but it was a night I had longed for in our relationship after being friends for a long time. We had both waited anxiously for the moment that would swathe us at night in one bed. She was ready because she agreed to pass the night at my flat. She had promised that repeatedly to me..

"I'll pass the night at yours. Not before then," she had told me.

"When will that be?" I had asked impatiently.

"Just be patient with me. I am not running away. You will get what you want," she had said matter-of-factly.

I then would imagine the cherry fruit falling for me when it was ripe. The cherry fruit only fell when it was ripe and only for its favorite to pick. In childhood days, we yearned for the bell-shaped fruit whose flesh and juice had such a wonderful and hallucinating taste. As a child, I woke very early to join the group that would race and arrive at the lone tree's shaded ground to pick fruits that had fallen overnight.

Time passed fast. Days turned to weeks, and weeks gave way to months. At last she was herself tired like me of waiting,

I believed. I had been more than ready to wait for her to be ready. I trusted her and knew too well that she would keep to her promise and come to mine the day she felt like doing so. Knowing that she was madly in love with me too, as I was with her, I expected she would not delay for too long to get intimate with me. The cherry fruit, I knew, would not wait for too long before showering ripe fruits on its favorite some early morning.

When the time came at last, it was a night she would not fully remember, but which remained etched indelibly in my memory. It was a night of revelation, a night of exotic tongues, a night of magic. It was a night my bed brought the known and the unknown together. It was the night that the much-anticipated consummation of our love took a turn I had least expected. It was a night I would not have wished for with such passionate longing. It was a night of a unique drama, and I was the sole audience. The cherry fruit would maintain its unique wonderful and hallucinating taste for its favorite.

❖ ❖ ❖

I did not know that Kena had another name. It came much later through revelation. Omotedjo. That was not a common name and I had not heard her called by that name. Nor had she introduced herself to me as bearing that name that defined her status. She was a graduate of the University of Port Harcourt and taught Fine Art at Okugbe Secondary School in Essi Layout, Warri. It was a school known for its neat and hardworking students; its principal and teachers very demanding of their students. I could picture Kena's drawings and paintings of female figures that could neither be described as exotic nor esoteric and an uncompleted portrait of a man. Many of the women had long hair, were rather bony and tall. Others had cropped hair, not as tall and were moderate in size. A white coating, as of kaolin, covered their bodies and they looked surreal. Once I met her at her art table, at the corner of her sitting room, staring at a work I had seen her before stare at for a long time without touching.

"This portrait is giving me too much trouble," she had told me.

"Leave working on it until the inspiration comes for you to continue, if not to complete it," I had advised her.

"I don't even know the man that I am drawing, but it possesses my pencil and yet will not lead me to have a full profile of him," I remember her telling me of the mysterious man that she spent time and time again drawing to no end.

I could not make anything of the male figure. To me, it was more of a shadow than an embodied person. I thought with time and inspiration she would come out with a definable male figure. I thought she was too anxious to complete a work that needed not to be hurried over. After all, the muse would assist her when ready just as the ripe cherry fruit when ready would fall for the tree's favorite.

It was after a long night that I knew Kena to be not only my girlfriend but also Omotedjo, daughter of Mami Wata. How could she be Mami Wata's daughter if her father was not Mami Wata's husband or her mother, for that matter, was not the water goddess herself? I asked myself. There were many things that I did not know and would know through my relationship with Kena, the lady I had fallen in love with at first sight and loved so deeply.

Kena was a very beautiful lady. In our riverine region, I had not seen any young woman who possessed such beauty and cool features. She had unusual elegance and femininity that were unique to her. Tall and of a moderate size, she was just only one special beauty; alone in her class.

We had agreed to be friends but did not know each other intimately for a long time. I believed she wanted to study me and I too wanted to study her. At first I thought she wanted to hold back for as long as she could in order to kindle more my

passion for her. I didn't mind that. I worshiped her. If someday
we would marry for life, getting familiar should take some time,
I believed. We did not know that getting to know each other
well would bring us so many problems and eventually tear us
apart.

Both of us understood that we had to exercise restraint,
believing that, once we started making love, we would have a
surfeit of it. So, why hurry to where we were going to spend the
rest of our lifetimes together? I asked myself in reflection, since
both of us were quite young. She was twenty-six and I twenty-
eight. She was young, fresh, and dazzlingly alluring. I had Kena
on my mind when she was not with me and was dazed by her
beauty while she was around.

Kena visited me in the late morning on weekends. Then
her beauty bristled. She had a silken skin with the complexion of
boiled palm oil that many of us men sought in women. I knew
the Great Maker was generous with his flawless talent in crafting
her. No human being could be better sculpted than she who had
possessed me with her charm.

"This is for you," she would tell me. "I know you will like
it," and she gave me whatever she got for me.

She did not earn much, but she made sacrifices, as I saw it,
to express her love for me. Now she would buy me a shirt, then
singlet, socks, and handkerchiefs. I reciprocated, but not to the
extent of her care, kind heartedness, and remembrance of me.
I once bought her a perfume that Hausa traders hawked. It was
well packaged and smelled so well. She appreciated it and would
wear that perfume the night she would come ready for me. I was
blown away whenever she put it on.

She often teased me, and that was what she did on one of
her visits to me while we held each other's hands as we sat on the
two-seater in my sparsely furnished apartment.

"One man working with Shell tried to toast me today," she
told me.

"And what happened?" I asked.

"Of course, he was wasting his time. I have got my love. It's you and I don't need to care about any other man," she explained coolly.

"You are a terrific lady!" I complimented.

She was the lone fixed star in my firmament. I had no anxiety over our love that was solidly based on trust in each other.

When Kena visited me, she left before dark for home.

"I don't want to be out late," she always said.

There was something in darkness, I thought, she feared. Of course, I could understand why a young woman would not walk the streets of Warri in the night. There were many bad boys that could be a nuisance once they were invisible in the dark. I lived on Radio Road; she lived on Igbi Street. We lived about five kilometers apart. Those five kilometers at night had many area boys who tested their prowess by the number of people they robbed or the girls they raped.

Also when I visited her, I left before it was late. Besides, none of us wanted our parents or friends to think that we had gone farther than we really had in our relationship. We would go slowly before plunging into intimacy with abandon, if that was what staying together alone at night meant.

One day I was carried away with our cheerful chatting and stayed till a little late at her place. Her mother was visiting and, from the look of things, was going to spend the night at hers. It was past eight o'clock. She was getting restless and behaving strangely. It was as if she was preparing for something that I was not going to be a part of. Or rather, I was slowing down the process of her getting ready for somewhere or getting something done. I could not read exactly what was different in her, but her manners were very surreal.

"Will you like to accompany me home?" I asked her.

"You know that won't happen now and more so as my mother is visiting," she said.

"Are you all right?" I again asked.

"What do you mean?"

"I just feel you are not quite yourself," I ventured to say.

"I am quite fine," she responded.

We both knew the time was approaching for us to spend more time together, for her to pass the night at mine. I would relish telling and sharing stories with her, as I would like to share hers too.

"Don't be in a hurry," she told me again.

"When you are ready, I will be ready," I said.

I knew that she would soon be ready for me. I imagined the cherry tree would not hold back for too long again before showering its ripe fruits on its favorite.

* * *

Kena was the first to go to bed. She put on her pink lingerie that made her a sexy goddess in a human incarnation. She had a knack for selecting dresses that fitted her perfectly well. It was as if the seamstress or whoever sewed the sleeping gown measured her body specifically for it.

"You look great," I complimented.

"Thanks," she replied.

She was rather coy, perhaps because it was the first time that I saw her in a sleeping dress. Her profile came through in the half-transparent gown, which confirmed her charming features.

"Let me relax a little before you come to bed," she said, as I watched the network news at nine o'clock.

If she chose to go to bed before me, no problem, I thought. I obeyed her wishes as she also obeyed mine. I thus saw no need to go to bed with her at the same time when she wanted to be in bed first and be alone for a while before I joined her. If she was ready, and we had been waiting for that moment for two years, a half hour was no problem. I thought there was some trepidation in her mind about sleeping with me for the first time. I also had my anxiety but was ready to go through the suspense of seeing her naked, as she would also see my naked body.

After she left, I went to the refrigerator for a bottle of Gordon's Spark, my favorite drink. I sipped it as the television news went on. As usual, the NTA reported the giant strides of the military government. Are these newsmen and women living in another world or in what world were those achievements they attributed to the military regime? I asked myself, comparing the devastated country that the soldiers were still plundering with the Nigeria of the NTA news reports. But my mind soon came back to my sweetheart. The drink surely calmed me considerably and made me ready to go to bed. I put on my own pajamas, no comparison to the knockout quality of her sleeping dress.

By the time I went to bed, Kena was a different person. A certain halo hovered over her but soon cleared into darkness. I switched on the blue light, which reflected on her pink dress to momentarily produce rainbow colors that soon disappeared, as if covered by a dark cloud. Seeing her not moving or talking, I switched on a bright white light. In the blue and white colors she appeared divine but was already far gone into another world, very oblivious of my action to spy on her lush body. Her dark long eyelashes shone; the eyes themselves closed. I was already swelling with desire before I entered the bed. I turned off the lights because I did not sleep with them on. It was then that I experienced the unforgettable moments of my life.

Kena, totally unmindful of my lying beside her, was having a dialogue in the Ughievwen dialect of Urhobo with someone I could not determine. That dialect had a sing-song quality to it and could be very sexy. It was a boisterous conversation and Kena talked excitedly. I switched on the white light again. Her eyes remained closed but her lips moved in a rhythmic wave beneath her oval face. It was as if a power beyond her moved the lips in consonance with her words. It was like the sweet voice of a singer from a gramophone. She was so possessed in that state that she went on chatting, or rather prattling, for hours, as I watched her and almost forgetting that I wanted to make love with her. Was there a quarrel between her and the other person? Were they making declarations of love? I could not understand the meaning of the long and vivacious conversation.

At a point, I shook Kena to awaken her to my presence. It was to no avail. Hard as I shook her, she did not respond to me. Her body was just there but her feelings and spirit were somewhere else. I could not make love with her, unless she was aware of me. Or did she have another friend or partner, who was chastising her for sleeping in another man's bed with her provocative lingerie and perfume? I would never know that night what was transpiring before my very eyes.

I fondled her breasts, but there was no indication that Kena felt me. The few times I had done that before, she had giggled and looked at me with longing and said, "Don't go too far?" I touched her where, during the day, she said was her weak spot, but there was no reciprocal expression of feeling for me. I attempted to kiss her, but that was meaningless to one engaged in a conversation with a spirit she cherished more than me, I thought.

I observed that Kena spoke more fluent Ughievwen now than she did during the day when she spoke more of the standard language which I also spoke. There were no English words as if whomever she spoke to understood no English and they wanted to keep me out of their secret chat. She was rhetorical and appeared to be humorous. She even laughed at some points. But it was like the echo of laughter from somewhere else, as if she was near and yet far away. Her possession by the spirit was complete because she could not respond to me beside her. I was jealous of an invisible man, or whoever that person was, who was getting the better side of the woman I called my girlfriend and I wanted to marry.

Soon I was transfixed in bed, unsure whether to get up and go and sleep in the sitting room or hold to Omotedjo and wake her from the reverie, nightmare, or whatever she was going through at my expense. I chose to stay with her on the same bed in which I was totally ignored. Then I turned off the bright light. I had seen enough in many wakeful hours of the night.

At last there was a cockcrow. It must have been about four-thirty. Others followed. Kena said goodbye to the invisible companion no doubt and woke or rather came to her normal consciousness. Her altered personality seemed to have disappeared. Almost immediately the body heaved, became warmer, and my body instantly warmed up to her. I could now feel her heartbeat and breathing rhythm, fast in excitement.

She seemed to be aware of what she had done to me. She apologized and said she had fallen asleep immediately she hit the bed and overslept. She was a heavy sleeper, according to her. She might have only partly understood what she had been involved in, I thought.

I was still scared of her and was not in the same mood as I had brought to bed. But her body had changed——she became the Kena I knew; soft sexy voice, warm touch, and all that made her special to me.

"Dear," she told me, as she placed her right hand on my chest, rubbing me downwards, "I love you."

"I love you too," I said.

My fear and suspicion were melting away. I knew she would not deliberately do me any harm. Maybe what happened was beyond her control, I told myself.

The ripe cherry fruit had fallen before me, luscious and sweet as ever. I had yearned for it, and once she started speaking to me and rubbing my body with her hand, I extended my right hand to explore the contours of her body. The fear had melted away. My body became warm and my breath fast. She was no longer Omotedjo of the night but the Kena of the day that I knew. We exhausted ourselves. We collapsed to our sides of the bed and fell asleep again. This time slumbering at day brought no distraction from nobody elsewhere. She was totally mine. She stretched herself fully relaxed beside me.

Slants of light filtered through the louvered glass windows into the bedroom despite the curtains. It must have been about nine o'clock. Daylight had dispelled any signs of darkness from the bedroom. "I am Mami Wata pickin," she began, after we woke. "My mother told me so, but I did not believe at first. I remember that she used to rub white powder over my body when I was small before I went to bed to keep any bad spirit from hurting me. She continues to tell me to wear white to bed but I have refused to do that. Big girls choose what to wear out or to bed," she said, using her two palms to hold my face and gazing at me.

"I did not realize that we were in the same bed till the spirit said goodbye to me," she explained.

I was scared and not scared. After all, she was telling me the truth of her experience. She must be trying as hard as she could to break from that invisible one, I thought.

"Don't be afraid. I won't hurt you. Maybe some day the spirit will give me a secret that I could pass to you, if I remember. He is very jealous anyway and would rather destroy me or you than give me up to another man at night. Day does not matter to him. All that happened last night has been blanked out. I don't even know, except that I was somewhere else for as long as night lasted and I slept, if sleep was what I had experienced."

We soon grew accustomed to the frontiers that she could cross but which I could not with her. I did not have the ability to keep off my rival, an invisible gentleman I could not reach to tell to leave my love to me alone.

Living in the riverine area, we had to contend with the forces of rivers, the Atlantic Ocean, and bodies of water close by. Kena's, rather Omotedjo's, lover was from the waters, I later learned.

* * *

My people recognized marriage only after the bride price had been paid. Kena's parents would not accept my bride price. I had gone to introduce myself to them and to propose a date for me to pay the bride price. Her father was nice to me, showed me to a seat in his large sitting room, and offered me a Coke.

After I introduced myself, I told him that I was interested in his daughter and would like to marry her. I would like to arrange with him when would be best for me to come to do the pre-marriage obligations.

"We can't take more than one bride price," her father told me.

"Have you received one from another man to marry her?" I was forced to ask.

"Her mother and I wanted you to get close enough to her and know that you are flirting with another person's wife. We don't know the person but there is somebody already in her life and possessing her. She will not be able to focus her love on another man as things stand. I believe you must have witnessed her at night. You can only be mere friends," he said.

"What do I do now?" I asked Kena, after I left her father.

"Does the bride price matter?" she asked.

I was silent. How would she want us to live together without my having authority over her as my wife and she having me as her husband, as customarily done? Should I marry a woman already married, even if that marriage was in a different world? What would she do if I wanted her and at night the spirit ordered her to leave me? I knew that Kena really loved me and was keen on our marrying. She must be trying still to get rid of the spirit lover, I believed.

It was at this crucial time of our relationship that I got admission to Syracuse University in the United States for my graduate studies in Public Communication. Kena cooperated with me to have her visa along with mine. Together with my uncle in town, we had gone to a magistrate court in Okere Road to declare that we were married according to native law and custom and were issued marriage papers. We decided to arrive abroad before letting her parents know. We felt they would be happy about our being overseas. But we did not know who would not be happy with our arrangements.

Once there, Kena had no contact with the spirit lover that was my rival for her attention. For the first time, she passed the night without the strange dialogue that I was getting accustomed to. Though it appeared weird, we made love for the first time at night. I was happy and relieved that Kena was mine and not shared between me and a spirit lover. I had nobody else or rival to contend with night or day.

But it appeared I was rejoicing prematurely about victory over a powerful force. This I learned from what happened a few days later. The problem we thought we had solved by leaving home behind for this distant place had not totally gone. Distance from home did not matter in this regard as we had thought. Or, rather, the new place changed our problems and threatened to wreck the relationship we were already celebrating as perfect.

A severe headache that paralyzed Kena emotionally took over within a few days of our arrival abroad. She told me it was as if a hammer was hitting her skull persistently once darkness fell. And darkness fell early, ensuring a long night. According to her, the echo and the pain of the hammer blows persisted all night. Neither she nor I wanted to attribute this occurrence to what we had fled from. We felt it was a new problem that could be resolved easily by the many experienced doctors around. After all, we were in America, the home of modern medicine.

However, every medical expertise we sought failed to treat the headache. Neither drugs nor counseling brought relief. She was referred to different doctors, who were said to be specialists in pain therapy, but the hammering of the skull at night intensified. It was as if an enemy was hammering her skull with a heavy metal and with vengeance. Once the hammering started, the pain spread from her head downwards and affected her arms, legs, and other limbs. She suffered from neither arthritis nor migraine. All tests for known painful diseases proved negative.

We had registered at the Carmel Family Clinic in Sycamore Street, where she had been examined and tests done. We went to see the doctor first, who addressed her as soon as we were seated in his office.

"Your tests show that you are a healthy normal person," Dr. Richardson told her, a point to be repeated by many others.

The doctor sent her to another section of the clinic to consult with another specialist. After about fifteen minutes of examination, Mary-Jane Allen, the pain therapist, wrote some things down on her note pad.

"It must be in your mind," she told Kena.

There was nothing she and other pain therapists could do to relieve Kena of the painful blows that afflicted her, but which medical tests did not catch.

Soon Kena was suffering from chronic insomnia. The pain had murdered her sleep. Night became a hell to her and we were scared when night was approaching like one dreading the appearance of a plague. It was the plague of night that she suffered from.

The problem was not what we could deal with on our own alone, we came to realize. There were experiences you would prefer to hide, but only if you could control them. The headaches and sleeplessness were wreaking so much havoc on Kena and me and destroying our relationship. We had to look back home for a remedy, if one could be found there.

We phoned home. Her parents wanted her back immediately, if I did not want to kill their daughter that I had eloped with.

"Yes, you eloped with her," her father told me.

"We decided together to come abroad," I explained.

"That does not make it different. You took her away secretly and thought you could live in peace with what is not yours," he chastised me.

I was being portrayed as a thief, which I thought I was not.

"Sorry, she is in deep excruciating pain at night," I also said.

"You should have known better that night falls everywhere, and not only in Warri. There is night where you are and what follows her at night will not stop with your elopement," he lectured me.

"What do we do now?" I asked, ready to accept his advice.

"She will die if you don't bring her home immediately," he said categorically and dropped the phone.

I had no alternative than to do as her father had ordered me. I did not want to be a murderer, killing my own love. I preferred to send her home while alive than be forced to repatriate her body should any bad thing happen to her. When she felt well at home, we could arrange for her to rejoin me again in Syracuse, I reasoned.

Kena appeared torn between staying with me with the excruciating pain and leaving with the belief that she would be relieved at home. I suffered the pain and the insomnia too but surely not at the same level as she did. I could never grasp the vehemence with which the hammer blows knocked her skull, much as I felt her pain.

We hurriedly made arrangements for her return. Kena had to fly back within three months of arriving in Syracuse. As soon as she arrived back in Warri, she returned to her spirit lover, as her mother told me on the phone. The night headaches and pain did not accompany her from America to Nigeria. I realized there were frontiers that could be crossed and there were others that could not be crossed. At home she slept soundly but in constant dialogue with the spirit in bed at night, her mother also told me. When I told her that I wanted Kena back when she was alright, she laughed cynically through the phone, and said "So you have not learned the lesson. We women here share one man but men don't share one woman." She must have told Kena this, I could tell from her disdainful laughter.

I grieved over the separation from my love but I was happy for her being relieved of the severe pains and the insomnia that could have driven her into a mental asylum and possible death in America. We were torn apart but we remained friends exchanging letters and phone calls until my friendship with April, an African-American lady, who did not want me to receive calls or letters from a woman she did not know. She had moved in with me. April and I were as settled together as a married couple.

CHAPTER SIX

Blacked Out Nights of Love

M UKORO NOMASO AND UFUOMA METITIRI were like cats over each other. Each threw away any feelings of coyness or inhibition to express love for the other. They held each other's hands in the street; they hugged openly. Their laughter was sizzling; their demeanor cheerful and vibrant. Neither had felt before now that he or she would ever be in love again. Each had been scarred and haunted with a traumatic experience, which repeated, could break any strong person. The experience of what neither felt would be possible again in life brought a new zest to their passion for each other.

Before he moved to Warri from Okpara, Mukoro had gone through many terrible experiences until things became unbearable. He had expected marriage to bring stability and happiness to his life. Rather, it brought him misery. There was no day without a quarrel at home; not just a simple misunderstanding between spouses but always a bitter one. His wife often started a quarrel out of nothing just to make him miserable and to hurt him, he thought. Sometimes it was after dinner that the quarrels started; at other times it was at bedtime. She often reserved her most vituperative statements for the time before they went to bed. She would clap her hands scornfully at him and begin her tirade.

"You think I would have married you if I knew what I now know about you," she would tell him.

The man did not know what to say in response to his wife's disappointment at his life.

"I didn't know I was coming to suffer by marrying you. You don't even look at your mates to see what they do for their wives," she would tell him, in a deliberate strategy to humiliate him.

Mukoro considered himself a moderate man, neither rich nor poor. He could afford his basic needs as well as his wife's but could not go for luxuries that would overstretch his budget. He lived within his means and did not borrow to buy what he could not afford.

"Things will improve," he would tell her.

"Useless man!" she would shout back, spitting out to register her disgust at marrying a man who was not rich enough to meet many of her needs.

On many occasions, she did not prepare food; nor would she allow him to prepare what he would eat. With time she slept outside their bedroom and from there hurled insults at him.

"You think when you paid bride price on me, you bought my body?" she would ask when the man started any foreplay.

She would tear herself away from the man. She avoided any physical contact between them. After some months, her sleeping alone became permanent.

After things had become so bad, they could not imagine having a worse time. At such a time, a solution was found. When an accident in the house claimed the woman's life, it was a painful relief to the man. It was a solution he did not want to speak publicly about.

They were having one of their usual late evening quarrels and in her rage she had slipped in the bathtub and broken her neck and died, according to him. In his account of what had happened, he did not mention the quarrel or the pushing which he had done. Outsiders were told she went to take a bath before they went to bed and slipped. From Mukoro's mourning for her, those who knew him thought he deeply felt the loss of his wife rather than the relief it was to him. There was no child in the marriage.

* * *

Ufuoma lived with her trauma like distressful underwear beneath a fine dress, which her church life and constant smiles had covered successfully, she believed. Or at least, they did for a long time. However, like a swimmer whose back was slightly exposed, Mukoro would peek into her past and see the ugly sight that he would toss away as not important to his relationship with her. He had seen so much that he realized that there was no spotless human being, including himself, and he was ready to deal with what he knew to be imperfect rather than what he did not know but was promoted as perfect. He also realized that however experienced a man was, he could still be tricked by a woman he loved passionately. When he peeked into Ufuoma's past, he was not worried by what he discovered. He was doing about the same thing that she was doing, covering up a sore past. And his deed was worse because he committed murder, whichever way he would put it. She was not responsible for her former husband's death but was a victim of societal prejudices against women. She was accused of being a witch because she was unlucky to lose her husband in their first marriage night to a heart attack. He believed that the present and the future mattered more than the past.

Mukoro had been widowed for fifteen years and for a very long time had felt he would never marry again. His earlier marriage was so bad that he planned to avoid another. He did not want to have a repeat of what had happened to him. That would make him die, he thought at the time. He was a murderer, however much he hid the fact from the rest of the world. Still he went on to take the praise name of "Who is in a bad marriage!" to which, when called, he responded: "A great calamity has afflicted that person!" He would avoid that affliction that had made him grey fast. His eyebrows, nostril hair, and forehead had grey hair. He certainly looked older than his forty-eight years of age. Many people would think he was in his early sixties.

Ufuoma was in her late forties too, but she looked very much like a lady in her early thirties. Her tall and sparse body gave her a very elegant stature that was the envy of many women. She walked gracefully, a long stride after another, but never hurried. Her body was fresh to see. Her eyes were large and warm and she smiled a lot. In fact, she smiled over her past as she grew older. It did not take long before any acquaintance or friend observed her infectious smile. She was blessed with very white teeth.

She knew she had to meet the challenges of Mukoro's love. She was prepared to love him with her whole being. She remained in the teaching profession despite opportunities to work in the civil service or some oil companies around. Many times managers, who were knocked out by her charm, offered her a job which she turned down. She knew more than those managers that she would cheapen herself as one manager's mistress and would lose her job when the man grew tired of her body. A woman grows older and wiser and becomes cynical of men's gifts, assistance, and declarations of love. Ufuoma saw through the men's goodwill the intention to chase her and ask her for friendship and love. The men were not spontaneous but appeared to her calculated. They were giving or doing her favors with the hope of her paying back in kind someday. She was mature enough to know what the lecherous men wanted from her and she was not ready to pay them in kind. She was too smart for that. More so, love could be fatal. She had been a witness to it and would do anything to avoid a repeat performance of what had happened on her wedding night, if she could help it, and that meant staying away from men. But she realized that she was human and could slip in her resolution. That was how she saw her friendship with Mukoro.

After being friends for two years, Mukoro and Ufuoma realized that their love for each other had intensified with time. They competed to send each other gifts and letters. They soon discovered that once in love, or taken oneself to be in love, one was inexorably blown away by love's passionate winds. One becomes helpless when truly in love, they also soon realized. Love was smoke that could not be contained. It showed in unexpected acts and places. Once it took control, one's gestures were governed by it in an intuitive manner.

One cool Sunday evening, after a heavy downpour, after they had looked at each other with so much longing during the morning service, Mukoro went to visit Ufuoma at her flat on 10 Radio Road. Since he had not told her earlier that he would visit, she imagined that there must be something important that brought him to hers. After exchanging greetings, they sat in the lone two-seater cushion chair in the sitting room. Ufuoma got up and brought him a bottle of Coke, which she poured into a glass for him.

"I hope you are fine," she said, starting a conversation.

"I am fine but not very fine," he replied cryptically.

This left Ufuoma a little confused. She knew that if something brought him to hers, he would say it before going back home. He was a gentleman and would not stay till too late before going back. After a moment of silence, Mukoro cleared his throat.

"Will you marry me?" he asked, two years into their "mere friendship," as Ufuoma had liked to describe the relationship.

"Of course, yes. I will marry you," she answered.

"Thank you, Ufuoma. I am a very lucky man," he told her.

"I am very lucky too to have you propose to me," she replied.

They embraced and held each other tight in silence. Their hearts beat a similar ecstatic rhythm.

From that day they started to make arrangements for their wedding in the Catholic Church. Ufuoma was seized by panic after the engagement.

"Can a woman's bride price be paid twice?" she asked herself.

"Whom do you return a debt to when the creditor is dead and has no known heir?" she further asked herself.

She wanted to marry Mukoro and did not want anything embarrassing or secret to break out to stop the planned wedding. She would cover her back until both Mukoro and she had respectively pronounced "I do," she reflected. After then, any secret would even be easier to keep because she would be faithful to her husband more than one hundred percent. Still, voices within her queried her for not voicing what Mukoro needed to know. "Don't you think it is better to confess all now and be forgiven forever than not do so and be destroyed by a secret later?" another voice asked her. "No, you don't have to expose what is not necessary. Nobody, even if an angel, fully reveals everything embarrassing," another voice warned her. "Don't say I didn't warn you?" the earlier voice reiterated. "A successful marriage is a matter of luck and has nothing to do with the past. Pray to be lucky and do your best in the new relationship," came a sagely voice.

Ufuoma had no friends to confide in or seek counsel from. Her fellow teachers at Hussey College gossiped a lot and she knew that if she confided in one of them, her story would go round all the teachers in the school in no time. Her colleagues were all telephones without wire. Without being asked, one of her colleagues had told her to be wary of middle-aged men about to marry. "What would have made them wait for so long before marrying?" the teacher had asked her. And the teacher was from Kokori, the same place as Mukoro's late wife had come from and close to Mukoro's hometown. Was she indirectly advising her to leave Mukoro? She had learned that Mukoro lost his first wife through an accident at home. She pitied him for the loss of his wife and the fortitude to stay so long without jumping into another marriage immediately. But she felt also that the misfortune that ended one marriage would not necessarily be repeated.

Each couple will live their own fate, she believed. With luck partners from former relationships could do well together.

She did not confide in any person in the church either. Her friends could tell the priest to get his trust. After all, the priest had several times preached about people whose secrets had been leaked to him. In a community of parrots, Ufuoma had no one to discuss her dilemma with and still remain the secret she wanted it to be.

What happened to her twenty years ago still remained vivid in her memory. In fact, it was etched indelibly there where nothing could erase it as long as she lived. Though it happened in Yola so many years ago, memory did not set any distance between Yola and Warri despite being about two thousand kilometers apart; nor between then and now. She had moved a long distance away from the scene of the experience, which followed her wherever she found herself.

As a twenty-five-year-old bride, her thirty-three-year-old husband had a heart-attack on their first night as a married couple; only several hours after the reception party. Some strange illness that she still could not fathom struck the vivacious man dead even before he could penetrate her. It was supposed to be a honeymoon for them but turned into sudden grief that paralyzed her emotionally for so many years.

Ufuoma could still recall clearly the body of Otebele slumped upon her and how the body became cold, heavy, and rigid. She could not even shout but pushed the incubus of a corpse from her top. The body was beginning to stifle her with its weight.

When the news went out later, the man's relations in Yola called her a witch, which she denied to no avail, as far as they were concerned. She lived with that stigma there for several years before she moved south to Warri. She easily got a teaching job and began a new life in her home state. Delta State would bring her good luck rather than the bad luck she experienced in Gongola State, she hoped.

But the back of the swimmer could be more exposed than he or she thought. That was Ufuoma's plight. She made up her mind that she would not tell any man who wanted her about Otebele. It was an experience that was better forgotten than revived through candor. She wanted it buried and totally sealed off her new life. She did not know what to say if asked about it. She wanted the past to be left to the past and the future to be a new life.

Unknown to the widowed bride of twenty years ago, the news got through thousands of kilometers borne by word of mouth hushed at close encounters. Mukoro had heard it but dismissed it as hearsay. Even if it were true, what had Ufuoma losing her husband the night of their wedding to do with him? He believed the man died of natural causes and the bride should not be blamed for the man's poor health that succumbed to the stresses and strains of wedding celebrations.

However, as the day of the wedding drew close, Mukoro felt his heart pumping more blood than ever. He was obviously breathing faster than normal. But he felt so committed already after the engagement and bride-price paying ceremony that he felt some demonic temptation was trying to derail him from marrying his true love, Ufuoma. He was also afraid that if Ufuoma got to know that he had caused the death of his late wife, she might develop cold feet and not go ahead with the wedding arrangements. Who knows? he asked himself. As he knew about Ufuoma's past, so Ufuoma might also have known about his past through gossip that he killed his first wife. But he felt the folks in Warri would not have heard the suppressed gossip in Okpara at the time fifteen years ago that his wife's fall might not be a simple accident. After all, he had moved from Okpara to Warri to put that episode behind him.

When the priest asked that anybody who had anything to stop the marriage should step forward and say so or forever keep silent, nobody came out to say anything. Ufuoma's late husband's elder brother, a drunkard, was there at St. Anthony's Church.

He had heard about the wedding and the elaborate reception that would follow. There was an opportunity to have free drinks and he came to the wedding to follow the celebrants to the reception hall for the partying that would give him free drinks and food. He had forgotten his errant younger brother's tragic end so many years ago. He and others in the family had refused to make the two-day tedious travel to distant Yola where his late brother and his friends had paid a bride price to his proposed wife's relations. Ufuoma's late uncle, who was brewing local gin there, had posed as her family representative to accept the bride price. The late husband's death had been taken by his people at home as punishment for his refusal to come home. None of them knew the woman he was supposed to have married. So his brother did not know, not to talk of say that Ufuoma's first bride price was not returned before the second one for this wedding. As far as he and other relatives were concerned, his brother was not married before he died.

The priest pronounced Mukoro and Ufuoma husband and wife, each given another chance to be husband or wife. Each prayed silently that the new marriage would not be like the first.

* * *

CHAPTER SEVEN

The Women's Final Solution

WHILE HER MAN VOLUNTEERS INFORMATION to her, other women are not as lucky because they are unable to extract any personal financial information from their husbands. She is said to be the only woman in the neighborhood who knows how much her man earns at the end of the month and yearly. The women know that she has a joint account with the man even though it is really only his earnings and not hers that go into it. She has a separate account that she does not share with her spouse.

Other women don't know how she is able to do this; more so, as she is married to an Agbon man like the rest of them. It is not only that her fellow women do not know how much their husbands earn but also do not have access to their men's accounts. They learn from the elderly housewives that the men fear that should the women know about their wealth, they could poison or kill them by any means and gain possession of the money. The women know that such reasoning, as killing their husbands, is just an excuse to hide their true financial situations and protect their egos because most of their husbands might not really have as much money as they would make one believe. In that case, the men keep their wives in a guessing game as to how much they are really worth. The women consider Lydia a unique woman in many ways.

"See her! She is called Lydia," Ufuoma says, as she points to her to Tobore.

Lydia dresses gorgeously and gracefully. She has a knack for dresses that fit her very well, and she draws compliments from women as well as men. The colors of her wrappers, blouses, head-ties, handbags, and shoes blend into a harmony that makes her figure a beautiful work of art. She has a good shape and she is pretty, but cannot be said to be extraordinarily beautiful. There are women who are more beautiful than her but do not draw to themselves the lust of men and the envy of women as Lydia does. She exudes the composure and confidence of a woman who gets what she desires. She is tall and on the slim side. She walks like a model in a rather coquettish manner that the other women cannot imitate however hard they try.

The women, also married, who point to her, do so without bitterness and malice. They don't know what to make of her— condemn her or be like her. But it is very difficult, if not impossible, to live Lydia's lifestyle, they know. She who can tame men, they call her. After all, their men are like goats on heat. They return to her, the men she makes friends with. Also, she is the one who commands men and gets from them her desires. She is more like a man in the patriarchal society in which the men dominate the women. She dominates. In fact, some women gossip that she always stays on top of men, what they will like to do but cannot prevail upon their men to do without being called prostitutes. Nobody, man or woman, dares call Lydia any nasty names. She is the lady who must be complimented.

Lydia is married, yes, but she is as free as, if not even freer than single women. Umukoro, her husband, works offshore for Chevron, the second most important multinational oil company in the country after Bell Oil that has been operating there for over four decades. A safety expert in offshore rigs, he earns a hefty sum and lavishes his salary on his flamboyant wife, according to gossip. She lives well, whether her husband is around for the two weeks he takes to spend at home or on duty at the oil rigs offshore for six weeks. His is a dangerous work and he is paid very much for it.

Her partner, as she often calls him, dotes on her. She is much younger than him; fifteen years separate them. He flaunts her like a prized trophy wherever they go together. He wears the same fabrics she wears, though sewn in their respective male and female styles. He takes her to parties and there are many, especially on weekends when he is back from the sea. He takes her to nightclubs, where they drink expensive wines, dance, and make acquaintances. Often she goes on tirelessly. The more she dances, the more the energy in her becomes apparent. As for the man, he cannot cope with her inexhaustible energy at all. She often wonders why he gets tired so soon whenever they dance. After the man takes his seat, she dances on and has the opportunity to have other dancing partners. She no longer complains to him why in bed he sleeps facing the wall rather than her. She has to look for a solution to whatever problem they have, she tells herself, and she has solved many of such to her satisfaction.

In his partner's presence, under his nose, as the women gossip, at such parties, she signals to her men friends that she freely associates with. She dances with other men and asks her husband to dance with other women who want to dance with him. Other married women dance with only their husbands or close relatives and with no other men. They marvel at how Lydia is so free and comfortable dancing with strangers and does what will be scandalous to other women: holding another man tight in a dance, while her husband is seated or dancing with some other woman. Other women cannot come close to other men the way Lydia gets away with it. Her partner does not seem to mind his wife's rather flirtatious manners in a society where men are so jealous that they wish to tie a leash to the waists of their wives and concubines.

The women have been socialized to believe that their an-cestors or some spirit will strike them with afflictions if they come close to a man who is not their husband or relative. No-body has ever caught her but many of the women do not only believe but also gossip that Lydia sleeps with the men she fancies whenever and wherever she chooses. That is supposed to be an abomination, which supposedly draws the wrath of the ances-tors. Not with Lydia, who is buoyant and vibrant all the time. Why do the ancestors not strike Lydia with an incurable disease for her dalliance? the other women ask in their gossip group.

"How does she do it?" Tobore asks Ufuoma.

Ufuoma and Tobore are outside the hairdressers' complex by the Warri-Sapele Road in Effurun. They have both done their hair and are exchanging pleasantries before leaving for their respective homes.

"Have you not heard what is said about her?" Ufuoma asks in a low tone.

"I want to know, my sister," Tobore pleads, like one who needs to know an interesting formula that she will try for herself.

"I don't have her courage," Ufuoma says, more of a lamen-tation than a condemnation of Lydia.

She holds her breath, looks at Tobore in an intense man-ner as if to assure herself whether or not she can be trusted. She raises her forefinger, closes her lips with it, and drops it. She gives a long sigh that Tobore cannot interpret, but waits eagerly to hear something about a fellow housewife whom they look up to but will not openly acknowledge.

"If I do what she does," Ufuoma resumes, "I would have been caught by my husband or shamed for my deeds by the ancestors."

This she says with a tone of regret. She wishes she can do what Lydia does without repercussions. Why is she always afraid of the ancestors who are dead and gone forever? She asks herself this and other questions about her temerity over living freely.

Tobore waits anxiously. She believes, as a woman, she has to learn from other women. Marriage, to her, has been a big burden that she cannot shake off. Being single is a curse in the society, much as marriage is hard. However, if there is anything she can do to ease the burden or totally relieve her of it in a way that will not bring shame, she will go for it. She wonders in her mind how one can continue stealing without being caught someday. That is a skill that she will find difficult to master. She praises any woman who gets her wish, however secretive the pleasure comes to her.

"I beg, tell me, my sister," she pleads again, anxious to learn a craft she may find useful.

She wants to know how to use the craft of womanhood effectively. After all, that is what Lydia has been doing so successfully to the amazement of other women.

"Don't say I told you-o, but everybody knows her ways anyway," Ufuoma tells her.

"I will keep it to myself," Tobore promises.

"They say Lydia has the 'the dead don't see and hear' medicine," Ufuoma starts to explain.

She pauses a bit, inhales and exhales, and continues her gossip.

"They say she either met a medicine man who prepared it for her or she did it herself. She must have used the soil or sand from the top of a gravesite in some concoctions to bathe herself. She may even have done the strongest of the medicines, procuring the water used in bathing a corpse in the morgue before being dressed for burial to prepare the medicine. She may have made a special arrangement with the mortuary attendant for a good price to get what she wants. Once she has the medicine, she communicates with her lovers only in English. That medicine neutralizes the power of our ancestors, who don't understand English anyway! You see that her husband does not mind and nobody will catch her doing what she does because to her the rest of the world is dead people."

"That's terrible!" Tobore exclaims.

"But you need something terrible to counter our terrible situation," Ufuoma says, as if in defense of Lydia.

"I don't think I can do that," Tobore admits.

"It will not be so terrible to me if my man will dote on me and I can be free with my life as I want. Look at Lydia! She drives a First Lady car. See her Toyota jeep? Her husband has also built a house for her from his huge income. How many of us can compare with her?"

Ufuoma has given birth to seven children already, and has no control over the number she will get. At the rate she is going, she could have ten to eleven children before her menopause. Now she does not want her husband but still gives in to him whenever he wants her plus his secret dalliances. "My husband is worse than a goat," Ufuoma sometimes tells herself.

Tobore already has five children and her husband and his people expect her to fill the house with kids and noise because they still measure the wealth of a man with the number of children he has. Her last delivery was through a Caesarian section which was not a pleasant experience at all. The attending doctor had to resort to that procedure when he found out that she was very weak and could not push. She had felt she was going to die from that delivery, but thanks to the doctor's expertise and her good luck she survived with the baby. *I am scared of being pregnant again. I just feel I may not be able to make it through the next conception*, she tells herself. And yet she cannot deny her husband the pleasure of her body.

Lydia looks very appealing. She exudes sensuality with her body. Her breasts are still erect at thirty-eight. Her hips are as sexy as a twenty-eight-year-old woman's. She makes up and there is enough money to procure her needs. She has two children, five and eight; both girls. She has put a stop to her procreation. According to gossip, she boasts that she wants to enjoy herself without being distracted by pregnancies and so has undergone a medical procedure to avoid pregnancy. Such gossiping women even quote her words.

"Who enjoys pregnancy?" she often asks her fellow women.

"For me," she continues, "the nine months and the labor period are times spent in hell while alive. I won't like to condemn my friends to that hell."

Other women listen to or hear about her, amazed at her forthrightness in the open. They cannot let out of their mouths such utterances that really reflect their feelings. They cherish what Lydia says but are afraid or shy to proclaim it the way she does with abandon. Lydia is the bold one. She is the shameless one to the other women. She does not care about what others say about her but says and does what pleases her. To other women, who gossip about her, it is because she feels immune from ancestral repercussions. The dead don't complain. The living and the dead are mute and blind before her actions and utterances.

"She must be taking contraceptive pills or wearing a coil," Ufuoma tells Tobore.

Other women believe this. There was the scandalous rumor that Lydia delivered the second daughter with a coil attached to her forefinger. She must be using some devices to prevent pregnancy but it failed in that instance, the women believe. These women also want to be free of the anxieties and problems of pregnancy but do not know how to go about freeing themselves from the perennial obeisance to the whims and caprices of men who do not suffer the pangs of conception.

"My husband wants many children, but can't understand the damage to my body," Ufuoma again says.

"They always want more children, our men. I wanted only two or three but my husband started to preach why one must have many children," Tobore says in response.

"They all do the same. Did my husband not ask me that if I had only two children and if one or both died wouldn't I be a childless woman? I was not convinced but had to agree to have more because there was nothing I could do to stop him from coming to me to have as many children as God permits, as he puts it."

"The world is changing but our society does not seem to be aware of what is happening. We are still having too many children that we cannot adequately take care of," Tobore tells Ufuoma.

"Can't you see that our women are either nursing babies or pregnant?" Ufuoma asks.

"I think only Lydia has found the final solution. I think I will be bold enough now to enter a cemetery and take the soil or sand from a gravesite to be free to live my life the way I will like to. Or maybe pay a mortuary attendant his month's salary to give me a half bottle of that water. It is nauseating, but what can I do?" Tobore confesses and asks.

"Yes, women do bad things because of their suffering. I can do anything now short of killing my husband to achieve my freedom to control my body," Ufuoma tells her fellow housewife.

Lydia joins Ufuoma and Tobore by the mango tree where they are standing and talking. She has been chatting with a young handsome man, both smiling and looking free and happy with each other. Her husband has gone to the rigs the past four weeks and has two more weeks to work offshore before coming home.

"My sister, good evening," Ufuoma hails Lydia.

"Good evening, my sisters! How una dey?" she responds.

She is so composed that she does not care that she is with another man, whom she appears to be having a good time with and following perhaps to a hotel for more fun.

"Take care of yourselves. See you at our meeting on Sunday," Lydia says, as she waves goodbye and goes her own way in the twilight.

They hold their Elegant Ladies Association meeting once a month and will meet next Sunday afternoon. Ufuoma is a member of the association.

As soon as she disappears into the dark distance, the two women slap the palms of their right hands, as if showing solidarity with the bold one.

"I won't blame her," Ufuoma says.

"Of course, none of us should blame her. Why should women condemn themselves or one of their own for what men do without qualms or the least thought of us?" Tobore asks, concurring with Ufuoma.

* * *

The next day Tobore feels she has to do something. She will not go to the mortuary attendant nor will she enter a cemetery. She needs neither the odious water nor the special sand to change her lifestyle. And she will not go to a medicine man, many of whom are quacks and around even in the city. Her life, she suddenly realizes, is in her own hands. She can live the way she wants to live by practicing it. There is much she can do on her own. Without being shy, she walks into JJC Pharmacy on Ginuwa Road and asks for a packet of condom, which she pays for and takes home.

She knows that her goat of a husband will come to her at night and, without fondling, will like to charge into her.

It happens as she has predicted.

"I bought condom for you to use. I am having discharge and won't like you to be infected with any bad things," she lies to him.

"What is happening to you?" he asks.

"Do you want me or not?" she asks back.

The man is taken aback. He is not used to his wife talking back to him at bedtime.

"I will not wear anything," he says.

He leaves their bed for the sitting room to mull over his wife's sudden stubbornness, as he sees her action. He falls asleep there and saves Tobore from succumbing to spousal rape.

Tobore thinks of another strategy. She cannot tell her husband every night that she has a yeast infection or some discharge. He may soon conclude wrongly that she is sleeping with somebody else, which will bring trouble to the home. She knows that her husband flirts, but he will not accept the thought of his wife sleeping with another man. She cannot withstand the hell that will be let loose in the house.

She thinks and acts fast. She goes on her own to a private clinic in Ovie Palace Road to install IUD or coil into her body. All she wants is to start to enjoy sex without the burden of conception or the monthly anxiety of whether or not she will have her menstruation.

Her husband is soon happy that the infection is over. She holds him back for foreplay that he is not used to. She teaches him what to do and he follows this time, beginning to enjoy squeezing her breasts, kissing her, and complimenting her body. It takes quite sometime before she draws him to herself and leads him on. She moans as the man also moans, but the man does not know what has taken place in the woman he has lived with as his wife for so many years.

Their love life changes for the better. After about six months, her husband wonders why she is not yet pregnant again, but he keeps his surprise to himself. By another year, he can no longer contain himself with his fears or suspicions. One night, as they sat on the bed talking, a preamble to foreplay and sex, he holds her right hand and draws her close to himself.

"Darling, why are you not getting pregnant?" he asks her.

He had started all of a sudden, since their sex life improved, to be calling her Darling. "Am I the one to ask? Why not ask God, my dear?" Tobore boldly asks back.

He goes ahead with the preliminaries of lovemaking both of them have now got used to. She has won a battle and feels she will map out how to win the war at home that will continue to make her a happy woman.

* * *

Ufuoma decides to take her revenge on her husband. He comes shabbily to bed, often not taking a bath. She always goes to put warm water in the bathroom and tells him to have his bath but he appears too lazy to bathe or feels he needs to resist his wife's order for him to bathe before going to bed. He comes in a hurry, as if he will lose his erection if he takes time to get her ready. She is not happy with him. She has complained to him many times that he needs to prepare her with foreplay, but he will not change. If he will not change, maybe she has to change, she tells herself.

She starts dating a younger man who makes her young and excited. She prepares carefully to meet him at times they agree on. She selects her best dress and provocative perfume to wear for the tryst. The day they first made love, the young man plays with her for a long time, touching parts of her body where her husband has never touched. She is ignited like dry leaf aflame in the harmattan. She is possessed once the man comes into her. She gets her first orgasm and a long one for that matter. *No wonder, nobody can stop Lydia. Nobody can deprive me of this anymore. I have now tasted the true fruit of love.* She talks to herself as one out of control of her senses.

That day at home she behaves strangely. The excitement, the sense of fulfillment, and her flushed body tell a story of contentment. Absent-minded, she seems not to hear what her husband is saying.

"Are you OK?" he asks.

"Why do you ask me that type of question? I am very OK," she replies.

She fears what will become of her if she experiences more of this special elation that love for the younger man brings to her. Must she go and prepare that medicine, which, according to rumor, Lydia uses, so that her husband and everybody else will be blind and deaf to her transformed being? She sings in the house as she is not used to doing. She fears she is becoming crazy. She has to do something to stop being caught or tormenting herself with fear of the joy she now experiences.

* * *

The two friends meet about a year later. They have started a new life that they hope they can enjoy without disruption. They promise themselves to go to any length to protect their interests like Lydia does her things. Even if they have to go to the graveyard to take the soil to prepare medicine that will make them free! Or pay the medicine man or morgue attendant to make the dead see and hear nothing as the living do what pleases them! But they will not go to Lydia to ask her about the potent medicine that gossip among many frustrated housewives says she has. She lives on so naturally, without other women really knowing the solutions she has chosen for her unbearable problem of having a husband who had become impotent and with whom she has made a devil's pact.

CHAPTER EIGHT

* * *

My Friend's Ministry

My PASTOR FRIEND AND I had dropped out of secondary school in the 1970s because our parents could not pay our school fees. We had to leave our Unoh village that was deep in the forest, where there was only backbreaking work without reward to do, and come to Warri, the Oil City, to learn a trade. There was plenty of money in town and everybody looked for ways to make it big. We dreamed big and hoped for miracles to turn our lives around. None of us wanted to live the type of life of our village parents who eked out a meager living. We were in town and wanted to live a real town life. And that meant having a comfortable flat furnished with a king-size bed, fans, television, and music players. With time, we dreamed one could drive one's own car and marry a beautiful woman and have children we would send to the university we could not attend.

As I learned my panel beating trade, Efe refused to do any type of work in which he had to sweat and hurt himself to make money. To him, that was not better than the types of work available in the village we had left behind. He was waiting to find some other ways of making money and living the town life we had dreamed of before leaving the village.

The first time he saw me wearing a mask, he was amused. I was already on my own with my own workshop, a shed in the panel beating part of Mechanic Village between Warri-Sapele Road and Ijo Road, a sprawling expanse of land opposite Warri Cemetery. The Village was the section of town that the local government council apportioned to us, according to its chairman, to keep Warri neat. All types of car-repairing work were done in the Village, and plenty of junk littered the area. Each worker had his zinc shed for his special type of work.

My shed was cluttered with pieces of car body parts. One hot afternoon as I was shoving the gas cylinder to the corner to give me more space to flatten a twisted passenger-side door of a Peugeot 504, I heard Efe's voice. He was much taller than me, even though thinner. I could always recognize his booming voice from a thousand voices. I turned to greet my good friend standing before me.

He stared at me with wonderment. I guessed he was going to say something funny, and he did.

"Wetin you dey wear? You don become masquerade for town or wetin?" he asked.

"No, na for my job-o. As the fire dey burn, I cover my face make my eyes no blind," I explained.

"I no fit do this kind job-o. Na killing job you dey do. One day you go burn yourself or you go become blind like Babi y'Allah when dey beg for road. No be the same town you dey with people when they drive fine fine car? Na you sabi," he commented.

He was not done with teasing me. He drew me out of my shed to show me some other mechanics.

"I think you see why we no fit tell madmen from mechanics for Warri?" he asked.

"Nobody choose to do this hard work. Life is hard for everybody here and it's better to do dirty work than to be an armed robber!" I answered.

With time Efe would get used to my work clothes and stop mocking me. I knew he felt a genuine sense of concern for me because sometimes I was really scared by the flames I used in working. The gas cylinder was also dangerous and had exploded once, after it had leaked out gas that easily caught fire when a cigarette smoker came to the workshop. It took me time to get used to working with gas and fire.

Before long, my friend was in a big church assisting a reverend, who had a large congregation. He followed Reverend Gabriel Okpako, a clean-shaven man in his early fifties, to retreats, prayer meetings, and evangelization trips in and outside Warri. He carried the reverend's briefcase and big Bible as if he were his personal servant. Before I knew it, my friend, who used to share *weed* with me, had become religious.

The first time I saw him with a Bible it was my turn to mock him. He had come to see me in my one-bedroom flat in Essi Layout, a crowded part of town. After he sat down in the only chair in my room, I looked closely at what he was carrying.

"Wetin you dey carry? That na Bible or na Dictionary?" I asked.

"You open eye and you no dey see?" he asked back.

In Warri, we had learned to answer mischievous questions by asking back more mischievous questions.

"Which time you don become dis kind Christian when dey carry Bible dey waka?" I asked, mockingly.

"You never hear say the world wan end? Make you convert-o!" he exhorted.

He thought for a moment.

"You wan die before you know say heaven dey? By then e go be too late-o," he told me.

"No be hell I dey now? Which kind hell go worse pass this one?" I asked, thinking of the heat in my shed and the fire I worked with on a daily basis.

"That is why you must convert and join God pickin," he said.

"So I no be God pickin now?" I asked.

"You must go to church to be true God pickin," he said, as he held out a cross from his pocket.

Six months later, he came to my workshop to tell me that he was trying to form his own church. He dressed simply, a white T-shirt and black trousers with a pair of modest black shoes. He now wore a gold chain with a cross. He was sober and calm. I realized that his service to Reverend Gabriel Okpako had made an impact on him. He was a changed young man.

Efe chose to stand rather than sit on the bench I wiped with a rag for him to sit.

"Bros," he started. He called me Bros, because we saw ourselves as brothers; we had shared a similar fate in the village— our fathers marrying more wives and not paying our school fees; later his mother died and mine too, leaving us to the harsh treatment of stepmothers.

"I wan change my life," he said and paused, calm as I had never seen him before in our long friendship. He appeared to have taken a deep breath and exhaled.

His face used to be creased with tension. It was now smooth. He also used to be unsure of himself and whatever he wanted to do. Now there was conviction in his voice.

I kept quiet and wanted him to say more about the change he was expecting that I thought was already taking place in him.

"I don form my own church and I wan make you as my best friend know wetin I dey do," he told me.

I felt humbled that he trusted me to such an extent as to tell me this major decision in his life.

"Thank you," I told him, unsure of what to say next.

Many questions came to my mind. How did this come about? Is it for real? Is it God's or money's calling? I suppressed those many disturbing questions for a simple one.

"Wetin be your church name?" I asked.

"Garden of Eden Assembly of God," he said.

"Make God help you do your work well-o," was all I could say.

"Amen!" he intoned.

That was a year ago.

* * *

I continued my mechanic work in Warri and knew how to panel beat accident cars. After my panel beating, the cars were sprayed and they always looked like new, not the *tokunbos* they had been before the crash. Some of my customers asked me why I had not gone to Kaduna to work for Peugeot Automobile Company to make cars with good bodywork, unlike the shoddy ones they were producing at an exorbitant price.

My friend's church grew. The Garden of Eden Assembly of God expanded from four people to ten, then twenty, forty, seventy-five, and now over three hundred regular people made the congregation. Members of the congregation testified as to how their lives had changed since Pastor Efe had blessed them. I did not attend the church, but we continued to visit each other often when we were free.

Two weeks ago, I visited my pastor friend, who had moved into a three-bedroom flat with a large sitting room in a new area of Warri close to his church. Pictures of Jesus Christ, Martha and Mary Magdalene, and many saints adorned the wall. The flat was comfortably furnished; a beautiful brown rug made visitors remove their shoes before entering the sitting room. He had fine leather sofas and a music player system. It appeared he played religious music all the time; at least that was what it seemed to me while I was there.

It was in his beautiful sitting room that my friend received members of his congregation and others who had heard about him and came for counseling and advice on how to solve their problems. He was not yet married like me. While I was there, Regina, or rather Mrs. Regina Tejiri, came to consult him.

She sat holding her feet together and not showing interest in the glass of Sprite that my friend had offered her, and I could tell that she had a big problem bothering her. I wanted to leave and so gulped my glass of Coke, but my friend signaled to me to wait. I guessed he wanted me to see how he carried out his ministry. I sat to the left of my pastor-friend on the same sofa, while the visiting woman sat opposite my friend on a different sofa.

"Madam, anything I fit do for you?" my friend asked Mrs. Tejiri.

"Yes, Pastor. My marriage is in deep trouble, and very soon if things continue at this rate, either we will burn our house down or kill ourselves," she said.

"The Lord will not allow that to happen!" my friend said, as if reciting a chant.

"Every day that my husband comes back from work, he starts a quarrel and beats me. We fight almost every day and I don't want to see him again; he might as well die and leave me alone," she complained.

My friend struck the side table with his right fist thrice to register his protest over what the woman was saying.

"Don't say such words. A Christian should not wish even an enemy dead; you can pray for him to change to be a better person than die an evil person," he said, shaking his forefinger at the woman.

"I can't pray for that wicked man," she responded.

There was a pause, as if one was waiting for the other to talk.

"Madam, I will solve your problem with prayers but never wish your husband to die. Also, I have to visit your house and see some things for myself. When does your husband come home from work?" he asked.

"Between 5:30 and 6 p.m.," she answered.

"Go home and be a good Christian wife and have faith in Jesus solving your problems," he counseled.

"We must pray," Pastor Efe added, and signaled for all three of us to stand up.

I, who had looked on mute as he counseled the woman, stood up to pray with them. The prayer was brief.

"May God give us the virtue to live good Christian lives," he prayed.

"Amen," Mrs. Tejiri and I responded.

Efe led the woman out and came back to meet me. We ate a sumptuous dinner of rice and chicken that day, what we had wished for ourselves as soon as we had arrived in Warri. A member of my friend's congregation had brought the food. He told me he rarely bought food and that his congregation provided for him.

The following day, Pastor Efe picked me from Mechanic Village to go and see Mrs. Regina Tejiri at her place at 5 p.m., a half hour before the expected return of her husband from work. My friend wore a pastor's collar and I was in a t-shirt and jeans.

We were stunned by what we saw. The sitting room had not been swept; the chairs and tables dust-coated. The chairs had their cushions on the floor, and the center table dragged to a corner where it did not belong. Worse still, Regina looked unkempt at that evening hour. She tied a faded wrapper over her chest, her hair not made, and looking haggard. She might not have even taken a bath that day. The only child she had, a daughter, was running naked in the room. She was as haggard-looking as the mother.

Pastor Efe nodded as his eyes surveyed the cluttered sitting room that smelled unpleasantly. He easily drew his conclusions from what he saw. It was a sore sight to behold.

Mrs. Tejiri went in to take a rag. She wiped two chairs which she drew to a corner of the sitting room.

"Pastor, please sit down," she said, pointing to the two chairs.

My friend shook his head.

"Thank you, madam. We are in a hurry and can't sit," he said.

He beckoned her to the corner of the sitting room, where she had sat the two chairs. They stood, facing each other.

"Come and see me tomorrow at 11 a.m. for more counseling," he told her.

We left immediately. He told me to be around at that time. I thought he wanted me to know how he carried on as a pastor-counselor.

The following day, Mrs. Tejiri came to see the pastor. I was already there and seated when she arrived. Efe motioned to her to sit opposite him. He did not waste time before saying what he had for her.

"Always keep your house clean. Make sure you sweep the sitting room and arrange everything neatly. Scrub the toilets to a shine. I believe your bedroom should be the same—neatly arranged and pleasing to see. Also take care of yourself and your baby, especially before your husband arrives from work. Let him see you, his daughter, and the house clean and beautiful. God dwells in a neat house. You must do what I have told you.

One more thing! I will give you holy water. Whenever your husband comes from work and starts to quarrel, take a draught of this water in your mouth. Don't swallow it during the period of his quarrel; just hold it in your mouth. After he has cooled down, drink the water! Can you do as I have instructed?"

"Yes, Pastor."

"Then go. You will have peace in the name of Jesus," he intoned.

"Amen!" she responded.

❊　❊　❊

My pastor friend came to visit me, smiling, only four weeks after the counseling session with Mrs. Tejiri. He came to me in Mechanic Village. Up to the time he came in the late afternoon,

I had had no job to do. It was one of those days that I just fid-dled with my tools with nothing to do. I asked my friend to sit on the bench I had there. I wanted to ask about Mrs. Regina Tejiri because I had been wondering what had happened to her marriage, but before I could raise the issue, my friend smiled and tapped me by my shoulder.

"Bros, here is your share of the money Mrs. Tejiri gave me," he told me, as he placed a bundle of ten thousand naira notes on my right palm.

They were crispy, as if newly brought from the Central Bank. They smelled the freshness of unused money, quite unlike the dirty ragged notes with which customers paid me.

He then told me what had transpired.

"We both visited her house and I advised her in your pres-ence in my house and it is good you share in what she brought to me as a thanksgiving offering. She carried out my instructions by being neat with herself, her daughter, and their house. In her testimony, she told me that her husband has changed to a very loving man and he always wants her after work but sometimes she has to tell him to wait till after he has taken his warm-water bath and eaten the delicious dinner she prepares for him. She says he has suddenly become very kind to her, giving her plenty of money to go and buy whatever she wants and make her hair. When last she came to me, her hair was braided, and she looked so sexy. She is happy that I told her what to do and Jesus has blessed her."

We smiled. My friend was a pastor using commonsense to advance God's ministry.

"Bros, she also told me that she and her husband would now be worshiping in The Garden of Eden Assembly of God Church," Efe reported cheerfully.

"You are doing very well, my good friend," I told him.

"It is only by God's grace," he replied with humility.

We both smiled again.

"Take this! It is right you share in what she has brought to me, twenty thousand naira," he told me.

I wanted to exclaim at the huge amount the woman brought as her thanksgiving, but I stifled the thought. She must have felt very grateful for my friend's advice and prayers.

"Bros, do I really deserve this? Many thanks," I said.

"None of us really deserves God's grace. Bros, I told you that your work is too hard. Think about it!" he reiterated.

* * *

CHAPTER NINE

Nobody Loves Me

The handwritten note on the bed simply read: "Nobody loves me." A big nail cutter kept the white sheet of paper from flying off. The writer wanted the note to be read, it appeared, because of the clear way it was written and the effort to make sure it remained easily visible on a neatly made bed. There are people, dead or alive, who do not want to leave others guessing their personal intentions; more so, on such an important matter as love.

The shock in the compound and neighborhood was unprecedented and spread cold shivers to everyone who knew Ngozi or any of the other tenants. Ngozi was one of the many single young women who lived in this self-contained one-bedroom complex in Alaka Quarters of Effurun. Chief Kemukemu owned the residential buildings, which he had built with the windfall from a highly inflated contract to supply sandbags for military checkpoints in cities during the General Buraimoh military regime, which he defended and praised as the best military administration in Nigeria's history despite its blatant repression and corruption. Civil rights activists said that Chief Kemukemu was capable of selling his own mother to make money. That told how much he cared for money; he would do anything to get it, including singing praises of vultures and hyenas.

The chief specialized in renting his flats to single young women, who ranged from twenty-two to thirty-seven years of age. With three storey buildings of eight self-contained flats on each floor, the compound, well secured with an imponderable gate manned by a kola-chewing Hausa man, was a beehive of visitors. It looked like a hostel for rich university students. And the tenants lived like youthful students with the exuberance of those free from parental watch and stretching freedom beyond traditional limits.

Some of the tenants had friends, like them single, living with them. The tenants were workers, and mornings and evenings, as they went to and returned from work, the spacious compound was a parade ground of beautiful ladies. Some of them stood out for their features. Rather, some were popular, as one would expect in this type of place.

There was the stylish slim, tall, and model-walking Ebi that everyone acknowledged as a stunning beauty. She walked with a conscious gait and was as seductive as she possibly could to attract attention. Lola spoke with a British Cockney accent. She was born in England and her parents repatriated her to study in Nigeria with the hope that she would get a Nigerian man to marry rather than remain single in London. Her rich parents spoilt her because they did not treat her as a worker but as one who should be sent pounds sterling to live a comfortable life in Nigeria. Marho was known for singing religious songs. She was beautiful, but spent much of her free time and weekends in the Church of the New Dawn, where she hoped to get a man to marry. She expected whoever would marry her to be "born again" like her and they would sing hymns before going to bed at night and upon waking in the morning.

Ngozi was beautiful and at the prime of womanhood. She was already in her early thirties. At the University of Jos she had been a very sociable lady and was known for that. Ever since she completed her national service in Takum, Taraba State, she had calmed down, hoping to get a worthy suitor to say goodbye to spinsterhood.

Visitors kept the gateman busy on week days, but more so
on weekends. Men, young and older, were constantly going in
or leaving the compound, sometimes escorted by those they had
visited. On Friday and Saturday nights, in particular, cars parked
along the entire Egbo Street, and pairs of men and women could
be seen chatting before driving off or after returning from their
outings.

What surprised the gateman was that no man slept in any
of the flats. No man was considered intimate enough with any of
the young ladies to warrant sleeping in her flat. It was an unwrit-
ten agreement among the young women, it appeared, to keep
men out of their flats at night.

It did not take time before a pattern emerged of the visitors and those visited. Some of the tenants constantly received
visitors, sometimes more than two men at the same time. Such
tenants with multiple visitors or partners either stood or sat awk-
wardly talking to their friends, as if each of the visitors was not
aware of the other visitor's relationship with them.

A few of the ladies did not receive visitors at all and some
did occasionally, even as there was the heavy traffic on a daily
basis. The gateman and the landlord praised those young women
who did not subject themselves to immorality or sex trade, as
they saw the nightly transactions. Ngozi and Marho were two
of such, often contrasted with Lola and Ebi, whom they called
shameless prostitutes.

The gateman overheard many things and saw much drama
that he kept confidential. Sometimes he listened to the haggling
going on just beside the gate, where he sat waiting to open or
close it. He usually spread out a mat by the side where he sat,
watching.

"This money is not enough!"

"That's all I have with me," the man would reply.

"Why did you not tell me you had no money before I followed you," the young woman would reprimand the man.

"You be meat I dey buy or wetin you think you be?"

"How you no go talk nonsense? You don get wetin you want," the lady would say.

She would wave her forefinger.

"Don't do this to me again. I am not cheap," the woman would add.

The young women looked prosperous as they had expensive electronic gadgets in their beautifully furnished rooms. Many had plasma television sets and cable service that they could not afford with only their salaries. Each knew that their boyfriends had to "foot the bill" for whatever they wanted. They bought expensive dresses from what they were given by their men. Many were not satisfied with only one man but had to date multiple partners to live well enough to outshine others in the tacit competition that took place in the complex.

On weekends, many of the ladies came from outside drunk and barely knowing their flats from others. Some ran into their bedrooms and vomited into their toilets. They smelt of Guinness Stout, hard liquor, and strong wines. It was a boisterous atmosphere in which they looked happy.

In the two years he had been hired to guard the place, Haruna had noticed the young women change their tastes in fashion. At the beginning, they dressed in mini skirts and sleeveless blouses. The spaghetti blouse was in vogue. Many were even half-naked. Lola and Ebi flaunted their bodies, especially their legs and breasts, and appeared looking for handsome or rich men to launch them at.

However, in recent times, the women were changing, as was their taste in dressing. Many were consciously or unconsciously losing weight. He knew some jogged in the morning to lose weight and keep fit. Some that were plump had become slim in a sickly way. He had heard through rumor that some, despite the money they had, almost starved themselves to be slim because many men did not want fat women. Everyone wanted to be a "hot cake," as they put it in their slang, and so they had to be thin.

All of a sudden, many of the girls were wearing long dresses, almost covering themselves in jeans trousers and long-sleeves. Some literally wrapped themselves and could barely be recognized. A few wore dark glasses at all times. It was a riot of fashion, Haruna observed, as he manned the big gate.

He had also observed other young women who returned sick from clinics, where they might have gone to commit abortion after appearing plump and obese. Others suffered from infections and their regular visits to clinics told their condition. Condoms often littered the compound or the backyard where the chief planted flowers and kept some loveseats. Marho realized she was living in Sodom and Gomorrah, but felt she could control herself from not slipping into the immorality she observed surrounded her. She sang her church songs to remain strong in the adulterous environment, as she realized where she lived had become.

By the fourth year of Haruna's watch, some young women were very ill and a few others dying from unknown diseases. Still the floodgate of men remained open. Nobody mentioned HIV or AIDS, as if doing so would make one get infected by the dreaded disease. But the landlord and the gateman observed that those girls dying like malnourished figures and coughing into their handkerchiefs must be infected by the unmentionable disease. After all, these young women were all workers and they had men friends who took them to expensive restaurants and hotels and so were not starving to lose weight at that alarming rate. The number of the popular ones was diminishing, almost month by month. Some did not die there but went home and never came back. Since they paid rents on a yearly basis, the landlord was not bothered by absences until the rents were due.

Still Ngozi, for reasons she could not understand, received no visitors in a town of goats on heat. How could one live in Sodom and Gomorrah and not be approached for sex? she wondered. It bothered her immensely. She bought new clothes sewn fashionably. She even wore attractive dresses and paraded Egbo

Street nearby, but no man beckoned or talked to her. "What is wrong with me?" she asked herself.

When Ngozi attempted to chase one of the men she felt was loitering to talk to any woman he saw, she did it so clumsily that the man walked away. But also, unfortunately for her, one of her fellow tenants saw her trying to chase her man.

"Na my man you wan take? You no fit get man for yourself?" Vicky asked Ngozi, who felt ashamed of herself.

"Sorry, I was trying to ask him whom he was looking for," she lied to Vicky.

"Just be careful with other people's men," Vicky admonished her.

From that night Ngozi could not sleep well. She thought of her condition. "Am I not a woman?" she asked herself.

She looked into the mirror in her bathroom after stripping. She looked at her eyes, lips, breasts, face, and all parts of her body. She was not an ugly woman, she assured herself. Her eyes twinkled and she cropped her eyebrows at the salon. Her lips were thin and they looked fine when she put on lipstick. She had full-size breasts that many ladies would envy, and she went for the most expensive imported bras in the market. Her face was oval and smooth, unlike some other ladies around with pimples taking over their faces.

Ngozi searched for a reason why she did not appeal to any man with so many men there seeking women. She knew that men drove round Effurun and stopped to pick girls on the street. She had walked, two weeks earlier in the evening, instead of taking a bus, but no man in a car stopped for her. She started to feel that she was not a complete woman or fate was unfair to her. Every other woman she knew in the compound had a boyfriend, man friend, or suitor. She wanted to be chased. She was tired of looking forward to a man and not having any; she wanted to make love like she knew the other young women were doing. She was tired of fondling her own body and however long and hard she did, it never gave her the pleasure that she expected from a man. She needed the warmth of another body. She wanted her body to be admired, wanted her expensive bras to be complimented by a man when she undressed for him. She wanted to be embraced, she wanted to be kissed, and, above all, she wanted somebody to share her life with.

She remembered that her elder sister was still living a spinster at forty-five in Aba. Is it true that the female children of her mother were jinxed not to have men? Did anybody place any evil charm on her to be loathed by men? An old aunt had died after confessing that nothing could be done to remove the curse she had placed on her mother's female children. Could prayers not annul the curse? She prayed and prayed, after which she went out dressed to test whether the curse was gone. Still, no man came to her. She had noticed that in her university none of the male lecturers had come close to her, as if she had a repulsive odor. She used designer perfumes but did not still attract compliments from any man.

From gossip in the housing complex, she had heard that a particular medicine man in a remote part of town made medicines for women to charm men. She constituted a court in her own mind in which she condemned and absolved herself.

"If you are a Christian, why would you go to a medicine man?"

"I need help because I have tried all means and failed?"

"Why do you think going to the devil will help you?"

"I won't mind if the devil will make me a complete woman."

Ngozi, on a weekend evening, when her fellow tenants were being picked up by men, took a motor bike to the renowned medicine man in a part of town without street numbers. Fortunately for her, the bearded gaunt man, reputed to produce the potent medicines for women to charm men, was in. After Ngozi had explained why she came to him, the medicine man prepared for her what he described as the most potent of the love medicines he could offer.

"Don't come back to tell me that every man wants you," he warned her.

"No, I won't mind men competing to have me," she replied.

Ngozi rubbed the medicine over her body, as she was instructed to do. When she went out, it appeared that she was having a despicable odor because men kept a distance from her. Those that came close by chance immediately walked away from her. Two weeks after she had paid the medicine man a hefty sum for the medicine that would make men compete for her attention and love, Ngozi had got no man chase her in Sodom and Gomorrah.

She started to lose interest in everything. She did not like the food she prepared. She did not buy food outside either. She picked any dress from her wardrobe and sometimes went out with awful combinations of dress, shoes, and handbags.

After the heavy traffic of the Friday, Saturday, and Sunday nights did not change her plight, despite parading like a real prostitute outside the compound gate, Ngozi decided to stay indoors. She knew that her mind was being destroyed by unfulfilled desires. She was not a lady, it appeared. She became weak and could not carry herself to work on Monday.

It was on Tuesday morning that her body, dangling from the ceiling fan tied with her wrapper, was found. The note was left on the flowery bedcover. "Nobody loves me."

Since she was dead, she did not know that on that very day too one of her fellow tenants died of an AIDS-related infection in the General Hospital. Also a few others were too sick and embarrassed by their sores and coughs to come out to ask what was amiss when wails rent the air upon the discovery of her body.

* * *

CHAPTER TEN

The Rubber Tappers' Fortune

No longer were people being laughed at as mad for planting trees in the rainforest. Rubber trees had become sources of great wealth to hundreds of hardworking men who had planted them and also to men and women who now tapped them for latex used in preparing rubber sheets and lumps. It was the boom years of the rubber industry, and many entered it to become rich. A pound of rubber was more than enough to eat well in a day, and most tappers made more than ten times that each day of work.

Akpo Vughe attended elementary school but could not go to secondary school because his parents were not able to pay his school fees. He knew he had to work hard to have any chance of becoming rich in spite of his lack of good education. He realized he had missed one way and he had to take another route, however rough, towards wealth. There weren't many ways towards a good life in Agbon; only hard work was the most probable one to his desired goal.

He started his independent life by tapping rubber. However, Akpo knew that would not be enough for him to make it and live the good life he wanted for himself. He realized he would have to get out of Agbon to change his life from that of subsistence to that of wealth. He thought of many ways to realize his dream. As he thought deeply about possible ventures to undertake, he decided to visit his uncle, who was a migrant worker in Okitipupa in Western Region, some two hundred kilometers away from Agbon. And so, to Okitipupa he went. There, his uncle Efecha produced palm oil, which brought good money to him, but Akpo did not want to climb palm trees and go through the tedious process of preparing palm oil like his uncle did. However, Efecha's money from palm oil was really not much, Akpo reflected, and his uncle was not a rich man in any sense of being rich. Yes, he could provide for himself and his family in a minimal way.

While still in Okitipupa and exploring what to do to become really rich, Akpo noticed that the Agbon migrants there were all in the palm oil-producing business. He also observed that there were many rubber plantations and yet no tappers. Did the owners of such plantations know what they were losing by leaving the mature rubber trees untapped? He asked himself. Surely, they did not, he believed. He returned home with plans to come back and join Uncle Efecha but to do what other Agbon people in Okitipupa were not doing.

It did not take a long time to put his plan into practice. Akpo left Agbon, where there were many rubber plantations and tappers and headed for Okitipupa, where his uncle had lived for over ten years. Not long after he arrived there did Akpo map out his strategy for wealth. He had to hire ten rubber plantations for five years at a pittance, compared to what they would have cost him in Agbon. He knew he was on his way to riches as a migrant worker. Though he could tap rubber, he was not going to tap rubber trees in ten plantations. He knew there was no man who could do that. He believed he could organize workers to make his wealth. He decided to go to Aladja to recruit young men, some of whom he had known, to tap the rubber trees and prepare rubber sheets for him. He would pay them four thousand naira each month and, after he had made his money five times over, he would allow the young men take two thirds of the amount they worked until the expiration of the five-year lease of the plantations. He took his entrepreneurial venture seriously.

It did not take him long to persuade ten Aladja young men to buy his business proposal. Everybody wanted wealth and these young men wanted to be rich and come back to do things at home. They would marry when they came back and build houses that would be the envy of their people. They wanted to be the envy of those who did not venture out of town or the area for bigger things.

"Life is a gamble," Akpo told them. "That is why the parrot dances now this way, then that way, and covering every direction because it doesn't know where good fortune lies," he added.

He had called all the ten young men to a beer parlor to explain his business plan to them. They were all seated, each with his preferred type of drink he had ordered. Only he took Fanta orange; the others chose Gulder beer which they drank from the bottle.

"Now is the time to travel far and get the money that is too difficult to make at home," he added.

They were already won over by the time they came to drink and seal the contract that he had explained to them. They acted fast.

"Level go change when we come back," the young men encouraged themselves, as they packed their things to go with Akpo.

And so to Okitipupa the young men came under the guidance of Akpo, in a motor truck. Efe, one of the ten, hoped that in three years or so, he would be financially strong enough to start building his own house at Aladja, and two years after then would return to marry Margaret, his sweetheart. Godwin, Tobi, Joseph, and the others had similar dreams of working hard

and succeeding in making enough money to meet the require-
ments of adulthood—marrying and owning a house. Both were
expensive ventures that would be hard for them to achieve at
Aladja, where there was no work and the cost of living was
very high. No longer, they believed, would they be begging for
money from parents and friends. Nor too would they be slaves
to contractors who used them and paid them with only food and
drinks. Life was just too hard in Aladja that they had to leave for
somewhere else to make a living.

Akpo provided them accommodation through his uncle
and took care of their feeding and still gave them what he described as "pocket money," in addition to the four thousand
naira monthly pay at the beginning. He set them to work immediately. The latex rushed from the tapped trees like a flood
in peak season. It was as if the rubber trees were discharging
the latex that had been in them for so long to relieve themselves of pain. The big cups were filled to the brim and the
tappers smiled at the species of rubber trees so full of latex.
Each of the migrant tappers could make seven to ten sheets of
Grade 1 rubber. Akpo allowed them to sell the lumps to add
to the pocket money he gave them. He believed in making his
workers happy. The boom he had hoped for was working out
very well. He got his money back much sooner than he had
expected. Within five months he had got what he thought he
would make in two years. He was happy and his employees
were also very happy.

The workers realized that they were making good money
and felt like treating themselves after the hard work. Money in-
toxicates, and the workers easily got intoxicated by the so much
money they had already made in the short while. As soon as
money was plentiful in their hands, they started to see beautiful
girls and women they had not seen when they had first arrived
in town as penniless servants. Now they were much richer than
the indigenes of the place that did not know how to tap rubber
and so lazed about for the lack of jobs.

The rubber tappers discovered Okitipupa had many beautiful young women they could be friends with. And with the sort of money they made, it was easy for them to attract the ladies. Godwin had got hooked to Toyin, Tobi to Kemi, and Joseph to Mary. They had suddenly fallen in love, and love was very sweet. After the day's hard work, they had time for their girlfriends. Efe was exchanging letters with Margaret at home, and both were writing sweet things that delighted the other. They would wait for each other and marry once Efe returned from his migrant work. He even asked permission from Akpo to go home during the first Christmas of their work to visit his parents and Margaret but was denied. He had to work and make himself rich before returning home.

"What do you have to boast of yet that you are so eager to go home?" Akpo asked him.

An astute manager, Akpo knew that the Christmas period was also the harmattan season, when rubber trees discharged so much latex that made the tappers very happy. He did not want the daydream of one of his workers to reduce his profit at such an auspicious season and he, of course, declined Efe's request. Efe's colleagues, who already had girlfriends around, also advised him to forget about visiting home so soon.

"Which kind love be that say you want visit Margaret from this far place?" Godwin asked.

"No be fine fine girls dey here or wetin you dey find?" Joseph asked him.

"Some people no know wetin good for them-o," another said, in an apparent attempt to discourage Efe from thinking of, not to talk of visiting Margaret in distant Aladja.

The rubber tappers had now become very visible in town. They spent money lavishly on girls. Many young married women also fell for them and there were reports circulating in Okitipupa that Ade's beautiful young wife was always smiling with Godwin who was not satisfied with his known girlfriend.

Rumor had it that Godwin and Ade's wife, Modupe, had a regular secret rendezvous.

The homeboys were inflamed by reports that the strangers, as they called the rubber tappers, were seducing their girls. They did not want their girls to follow these *kobokobo* boys who were there as servants. How could servants take over their girls and some of their wives? They took it as their duty to rescue their young women from spoilt young men from only God-knows-where.

"You will see blood if you don't leave my wife alone," Ade warned Godwin, pointing his forefinger at him.

They had crossed each other in the town's main street, when Ade turned back to follow Godwin to the front of the beer parlor in Ajanaki Street, which the rubber tappers always frequented to spend their money and treat their girls to the best meals and drinks in town. Godwin did not say anything, and that fueled the suspicion that he really met Modupe secretly.

The town was soon up in arms against these invaders. Meanwhile Akpo had himself impregnated a girl but denied he was the one who did it. There were many other pregnancies that the husbands and boyfriends of the young women now attributed to the migrant rubber tappers, servants of a servant.

What started as a little public irritant soon developed into a serious matter. A meeting of Okitipupa youths was summoned. Young men filled the Town Hall. Several old women attended the meeting, more out of curiosity than for any specific reason. The atmosphere was tense, as the youths felt something decisive had to be done to end the affront of the rubber tappers.

"If we don't do anything now, these rascals will take over our town and drive us out," Ade told a meeting of concerned young men in town.

"We have to kill them before they drive us out," Tunde said.

Tunde's sister had become pregnant and she had refused to disclose whose baby she was carrying.

"Let's burn their houses!" one of the youths shouted.

"Better to kill them than burn the houses they are renting from us," Ade said, surprised that he was defending the rascals.

Nobody listened to the counsel of the old women that the excitement would not last forever with these rubber tappers, the money-intoxicated ones in town. How they came about that assessment nobody knew, but they were very sure that the boom days would end for the charlatans, as they called the rubber tappers. The meeting broke without any specific line of action to be taken against the rascals who were seducing their wives and sisters.

The young townsmen got more enraged as many of their young women still openly went out with the rubber tappers despite their protests. More pregnancies resulted from their continuing dalliances. A civil war broke out among the Okitipupa folks and another war between them and the migrant workers.

◦ ◦ ◦

As predicted by the old women, the excitement started to wane before long. Nothing happened to the young migrants directly. However, what made them happy could, when afflicted, also make them unhappy. All of a sudden, the rubber trees became afflicted with a strange disease. There were no visible pests affecting the trees and so could not be sprayed with insecticides. The trees looked their normal healthy selves and had not become lean or shown any outside abnormality. But what used to be a flood was degenerating into a trickle when the rubber trees were tapped. The flood usually peaked during the harmattan period. By the second year's harmattan, the trees were anemic.

Akpo at first thought it was a bad season that would return to normal. He started to use his own money to cater for his workers, who could not tap enough rubber sheets to take care of themselves or save anything to send back home. But what the rubber entrepreneur had thought was a temporary phenomenon became a permanent feature. The rubber trees, for some reasons unknown to him and the tappers, had become a shadow of themselves.

The local girls and women were gradually getting less involved with the rubber tappers as their business declined. The flood had gone and the trickle was getting scantier and scantier. Some rubber trees failed to produce any latex at all when tapped. It was as if the trees were dead, and tapping them drew out no latex from trees that were robust with green leaves.

"These people don take *okpo* strike my rubber plantations," Akpo complained.

He had at a time cautioned his rubber tappers not to tap too deep into the trees. That was during the euphoria of the flood days. His tappers had listened and tapped the trees as he had advised and taught them to do. So he did not blame his tappers for the exhaustion of the trees. Evil ones far away in Agbon were punishing him for the money he was making, he believed.

There was no person to identify as responsible for what was happening. The price of rubber sheets had shot over the roof but there were no sheets to sell. At the same time the price of cocoa that had collapsed some years earlier started to skyrocket. Akpo decided to leave for home because he saw no immediate future for the rubber business among cocoa farmers; more so with sick rubber trees and luxuriant cocoa plants.

"If life outside is not good for you, better to return home," he advised himself.

It did not take long before the rubber tappers started to leave. This time, they left in groups of twos or threes, or singly. Only Efe remained to work in a cocoa farm. He had stopped writing letters to Margaret, who, his fellow workers told him, had married a rich trader in Warri. They knew it would hurt him but told him anyway about what they had heard from home. He was the only one of the rubber tappers left in Okitipupa to learn that the rubber trees were the first to fall victim to a strange pest. Soon the cocoa plants started wilting despite the heavy rains. He realized that an epidemic, caused by the appearance of an unnamable pest, was striking the economic plants, one after the other. He had to look for something else to do in Okitipupa, after making up his mind never to return to Aladja until he was rich enough and married to a local girl that he would take home.

* * *

CHAPTER ELEVEN

Married at Last

"I AM MARRIED AT LAST!" Margaret silently exclaimed, as the reception party closed. She had long tossed aside her parent-given name of Ese, the gift of God, for the foreign name whose meaning she did not know but felt it should be her proper name. From the way she danced with Victor, her husband, she expected something pleasurable in marriage that she had denied herself for so long. She danced not just with her body but with her heart and soul. When they danced together, one could see that she had more courage than the man by the daring and confident way she improvised new footsteps. When they tangoed, she held the man tight and swayed him this way and that way to the rhythm of the music. She was athletic when it came to "Sweet Mother," the music she had always loved and now swayed to like a possessed being. Her body tingled with excitement and she waited for the night to be with him alone and to share the joy of being husband and wife. It had been a long sacrifice, not knowing a man.

She had remained a virgin to this late age of forty-two because her religion proscribed any sexual relations outside of marriage. She had been "born again" since her mid-twenties, after she had resisted every effort by men to seduce her to bed.

At first she was busy with her education. She did not want to be distracted from her reading by any boyfriend or man. She told the men, who wanted her and said they were in love with her, that she was not yet interested in love. Most importantly, she wanted to be a self-reliant woman who would be educated enough to take care of her parents without a man's help or approval. She went to the university and got a degree in education, which qualified her for a teaching position in a secondary school in Warri. She hated abortion and did not want to have a child outside of marriage.

After she joined the Bible Church of Christ in Warri, she became very austere in her lifestyle—she wore no earrings, no bracelets, and no necklace. She cut her hair low rather than weave or Jerry-curled it as other young women did. She did not waver in her hope of getting a man, who would wait until they were formally married by a pastor before indulging in what young men and women were doing flagrantly. She knew that she was beautiful; not just because she was told so by the men who wanted her, and they were many. She saw herself in the mirror and knew she was blessed with a good shape. She was relatively tall, slim, and had a sparkling brown skin. She tried to be as cheerful as possible at all times.

Margaret had noticed that Victor always looked at her during service. He had formed the habit of sitting close to her or sitting where he could have a good view of her. He seemed to be not only greeting but speaking to her with his eyes. He had introduced himself as coming from Jos in Plateau State, where he had lived and worked for twenty-five years. He had considered Jos his home after marrying Rachel, a Birom woman. The Birom people were the major ethnic group in the multiethnic state. It was while still there that he lost Rachel, his dear wife. She had drunk herself to death despite his persistent protests against her drinking habit. Victor had been so devastated by the death of his wife that he could no longer live in Jos but had to return to his home state to start a new life. Anybody, man or woman, he told the story would pity him. Ever since he introduced himself as a widower, who lost his wife to drinking and he himself was a teetotaler, many of the marriageable women in the Bible Church of Christ had taken note of him.

"Here could be my man at last!" Margaret had told herself. She had heard about how Birom women drank *burukutu* night and day and the potent alcoholic drink made them behave waywardly. That was immoral, Margaret had told herself. It was bad for men to drink and worse still for women to drink and lose control of their bodies with men hunting for loose women to prey upon, she had reflected. Still, she would not pass any judgment on the dead. But she pitied Victor. It must have been a traumatic experience to have an alcoholic wife and worse still to lose her despite the bad habit.

Margaret was living by the rules of the Bible Church of Christ. She would not marry a divorcee because no marriage could be annulled once contracted. Only death could separate a husband and a wife. No court of law could do it. Marriage, she knew from her faith, was "for better and for worse" and she would keep to the Lord's injunction to the letter. The only option left for her was an unmarried man or a widower. At her age, she realized it would be very difficult to still get a single man to marry her; more so as men tended to marry early around. There was no man, she could think of, who was going to wait till he was forty-something before marrying. She had to be realistic with her chances. But much as she hated the prospects of marrying a widower, that was better than nothing if the opportunity availed itself, she told herself. And she waited patiently until Victor introduced himself as a widower.

At forty-two, she knew her biological clock was ticking away. Her body was already showing signs of changing and she suspected this could be the onset of ageing. Her menstrual cycle was becoming more irregular; the menstrual period itself very short—sometimes only one day or at most two days—instead of the four days that it used to be. What used to be a deluge had reduced to red stains over two days. She had to take advantage of her opportunity while it lasted, she told herself. She knew of no woman who got pregnant after her menopause, unless a miracle would make it so.

She felt free to endear herself to Victor. After all, he was not married and so free. She volunteered to help Victor in preparing *banga* soup. She knew how to prepare the soup very well. She had bought all the necessary spices, okro, other vegetables, and dry fish that she knew would give a master chef's taste to the soup. She used a traditional earthen pot to prepare the soup because she knew food prepared with it tasted better than one prepared with an aluminum or metal pot. She also deliberately used firewood rather than a stove. Firewood heated soup to be done in a unique way that the stove or gas cooker could not, she had learned from experience.

Once Victor ate the food, he became more lustful after her, she observed. They soon became the hunter and the hunted, each with his or her own aims. Victor prayed for everything and led prayers in the church. He was one of the lay pillars of the church and helped Pastor Ede in running the church efficiently. Soon Margaret became his favorite to be called to do things and she always obliged because she wanted to be close to him too. He wanted a woman who would be so committed to him in marriage that nothing would break their marriage. He could not tell how the woman he wanted to marry would handle their relationship, but he prayed regularly in private to God to forgive him for talking about Rachel, the drunkard Birom woman he had married, dying of too much alcohol.

He wanted nobody to either laugh at him or pity him. He was better off helping in the church and living the life of a normal human being, however things were with him. He did not want anybody to imagine him different from what he was seen to be—a good Christian man who was living by the rules of his church.

Unknown to Victor, Margaret had talked to some of her friends about a first night of marriage. She had gone to Warri Main Market to purchase a beautiful sleeping gown two weeks earlier. She had been avoiding sex but, once married, she wanted to throw herself into it. She had denied herself doing it for so long that she had to get a surfeit of it. Sex in marriage was encouraged by the church. No wonder in her culture, marrying meant having a sexual relationship. She knew there was much more to marriage life than sex, but it played a very important role in the life of the couple. She could imagine the ways the man would come into her. A few times in the past, she had been really horny and she had fingered herself and cried out as she had a feeling of exhilaration. That was the coming, women talked so much about. It was a sensation of bliss that she would like to have as many times as possible with her man. She was looking forward to as many orgasms as possible in her sex life.

Alone in the two-bedroom flat that Victor had cleaned to sparkle, it came to bedtime. Victor had changed the twin-size bed he used to have to a king-size one for the couple to sleep comfortably. Margaret was the first to get up from the two-seater couch, where they had been sitting and watching television before bedtime. As the anchorman ended reading the news, Margaret felt she had waited enough. It was bedtime. She held Victor by the hand and led him to their big bed. She made him sit on the bed as she stood before him.

"Victor, wait for me to change," she told him.

"I am tired," he said.

"Just wait. Don't worry about being tired. You won't have to be tired," she said, sure that she would rouse him to be vivacious.

She went into the wardrobe so as not to be seen as she changed. She put on the sleeping dress, light and transparent. From the dress, her breasts were full size. She had made herself as lovely as she possibly could.

"Close your eyes until I tell you to open them," she shouted to Victor.

"I'll close them."

She walked out gracefully from the wardrobe, a sensuous woman bristling with smiles. She was already warm and melting inside her. She felt it would not take long for the man to make her come.

She entered the bed and drew Victor to herself.

"I told you I am tired," Victor told her.

He got out of the bed and walked back to the sitting room.

Margaret felt like a deflated tire of a car in motion. Her warm body suddenly turned cold.

She was so naïve that the following night, she did not bother to wear the lingerie she had hoped would turn any man on. She came out of the bath naked and walked straight into the bedroom. After all, only two of them were in the flat and there was no need to be shy. She was now a married woman and she felt she had the right to strip herself before her husband. The more of her luscious body he saw, she believed, the more he would crave for her. Whether he was tired or not would not be an excuse this time, she thought. She was sexy enough to arouse him.

That second night drew a similar response from Victor, as had happened the previous night.

"I am still weak. The whole wedding preparations were an exhausting task. I hope I can recover from this," he told her.

"You are still tired?" she asked cynically.

"Yes," he replied feebly.

"Will tiredness prevent you from coming to me?" she asked.

"Let's wait till I feel much better."

After the fiasco of the third night, Margaret started to blame herself. Maybe she was not sexy enough. Maybe her age had made her not know intuitively what to say to a man. Maybe she did not know how to handle a man to be aroused to charge into her. She had heard other women's stories of how their men charged into them the first night and they made love several times. The men went on and on even though the women were tired. She had expected to be the one who would not be tired and she would goad her man on and on. Unfortunately, her man had not even tried it once to see how far she could go in the sex game of endurance.

It was a matter of time for Margaret to know what was wrong with Victor. Why had he decided to bathe separately from her? Why would he not come to scrub her back when she was bathing despite her open invitation? Must she tell him to come and make love with her before he would understand? She did not expect a mature man, more so a widower who had known a woman for many years, to be so shy about sex. Why did he wait behind at bedtime and sleep on the couch till morning and apologize for oversleeping there? She was asking herself many questions to understand Victor.

Since her husband was a widower meant he couldn't be a eunuch. After all, he had been husband before and must have been sleeping with his wife before she died of too much drinking. However, he did not tell her of any child or children with his late wife. Only God could bless couples with children and maybe God did not want them to have any child in that doomed marriage, she reflected.

After a month of the cat-and-mouse game with Victor and no sex with him, she feared the worst. In the past weeks they had been close together, there was no time his manhood swelled. Even though she had not been making love, but she had observed how men had behaved before her. She could feel the heat of the penis almost tearing through their pants when they were close to her. Victor's penis was too tamed to be normal.

She had hoped for a sex feast after holding back for so long, but she soon discovered that she would not taste that luscious dish at all. She was already married to Victor and could not leave him, according to her religion. "That's life," she muttered to herself, accepting her condition but not happy about it.

CHAPTER TWELVE

* * *

The Servant's Slave

EFETURI HAD ALWAYS BEEN VERY proud of his son and was tasking himself to educate him to become a professor some-day. But recently what he had seen of a professor that he once revered made him feel disappointed. He expected much more from a professor than from uneducated folks like him and his townsmen. But what he had seen over the political campaign period and the declaration of results without voting left a sour taste in his mouth. He sent for his son.

Tadafe answered his father's call. It was rare for his father to ask him to come to see him without something very important to tell him, the son thought. You could not be living in the same town with your father and not visit him once in a while. The old man's words of wisdom might rub off on him, Tadafe realized. He had come to the conclusion that if he could combine book knowledge with the canny wisdom of his father, his life would be very smooth.

It was late in the evening. Earlier in the day, there had been a heavy downpour, one of those late May rainfalls that made the people realize that the real rainy season had begun in earnest. Everywhere was cool; the air fresh after the dust of the dry season had disappeared.

Efeturi sat in his cane chair, his favorite seat in the parlor, gazing frontward, but not looking at anything specific. There was a meditative look on his face; one thinking deeply about the lessons of life he had not learned at his age of seventy. The son watched his father without saying a word. After all, his father had asked him to come and see him, and so waited for him to introduce why he had summoned him.

After a moment the father cleared his throat and went back to silence. He knew he had to talk. He wiped his beard, a preamble, his son had observed over the years, to thoughtful words from the old man.

"I called you here. Life does not always go the way one wants it to go," he started.

The son was confused by the riddle-like tone of his father's words. Was his father seriously sick and so wanted to disclose some secrets about himself to him, his only son for that matter? Tadafe was fearful of what his father was about to say, even though he could not tell what the riddling language meant. He did not look at his father's face but continued looking down, as custom demanded of a son listening to his father.

"You saw what happened the past two days. I have slept over it, but it won't go. It made me feel I made a big mistake sending you to school at all, especially to the university. You saw what Professor Tabunor Orere, our role model of a professor, did. It was nauseating and filled me with regrets about you."

"I also saw him, father," the son said.

"The day before yesterday Professor himself carried voting boxes stuffed full with voting cards he had personally thumb-printed as our votes, which we were denied from casting. And yesterday, he sat like a motor park tout on the hood of a party pickup drumming and chanting victory songs after robbing the people of their votes. He now sides with our enemy," the father told his son.

"I am not surprised, father, because he was made the Chairman of the Sam Temile Campaign in Ethiope East Local Government, and he accepted it."

"He accepted to chair an enemy's campaign!" Efeturi said languidly.

"I remember how he bowed to the gubernatorial candidate, much younger and far less educated than him at an election rally last month in our local government headquarters," Tadafe told his father.

"I heard about it from our people. Since nobody wanted to work with him, he had to physically arrange the chairs himself and made himself very cheap. Is he losing his senses or what is happening to him?" the father asked.

"I don't know."

"Maybe he was given so much money that he couldn't refuse," the father surmised.

"And I think he wants power too. He wants to be appointed a commissioner and so wants to boast to the successful candidate that he helped him win the votes of his people he has betrayed," said Tadafe.

"For sure he is now a slave to who should be his servant," the father concluded.

"He has changed," was all that his son could say in reply.

"If I knew education changed people to lose respect for themselves like this our townsman, I would have stopped educating you after elementary school. I would have sent you to the motor park as *agbero* and you would have risen to be the chairman of the Road Transport Workers' Union either at the local government or state level. You would still have had more dignity than our professor, a slave to who should be his servant," said Efeturi, shaking his head.

"Something must have gone into his head to steal his intelligence. Desire for money or power should not make this happen to him."

"Always have self-respect!" the father advised his son.

"I won't fail you," the son promised.

* * *

He was a very bright young man who won many scholarships to study up to the Ph.D. level. Though there were many in town with Ph.D. degrees before Tabunor Orere, he was the most impressive. The town's folks were disappointed that their brilliant son took up appointment as a Lecturer at faraway Bayero University Kano. They had expected him to be in the Midwest State University at Ekpoma to teach their children who would then turn out to be like him, a very learned man.

Dr. Orere was an acclaimed Marxist, who wrote in national dailies the need for the workers in the country to rise against their exploiters. He soon gained national prominence for his radical views. To his friends, he would always view things from a Marxist perspective, irrespective of commonsense ways of looking at them.

Midwest State was later split into two States, Edo and Delta. Delta State soon established its own university to cater for the number of potential students that could no longer be admitted into other universities because of the quota system. The new state had more young men and women qualified to read for degrees than the available universities outside would accept.

Dr. Orere applied for sabbatical leave and took up a visiting position at his home state's university. Though he was a Senior Lecturer at Bayero University Kano, he was appointed a Visiting Professor in his home university. Soon his friends called him only Prof and forgot about the Tabunor or Dr. Orere that they used to call him.

At home he was a phenomenon. Students loved him because he taught with so much zest and knowledge that made complex and difficult things easy to grasp. Colleagues loved him because he was affable and respected seniors and juniors alike. His people adored him. He was their pride at the university. Towards the end of his tenure as Visiting Professor, his appointment was made permanent. Now his townsfolk boasted they had a professor among professors and theirs, in their opinion, was the most brilliant professor on campus. They brought admission requests to him, and he was able to solve many cases by appealing to the Registrar and Vice Chancellor to assist, and they often obliged.

He did not wear expensive clothes but flew his simple shirts. He cut his hair at the local barbershop and exchanged pleasantries with the common people. He occasionally went to local bars to drink and chat with people. He was still an avowed Marxist, who supported the revolution of the proletariat that he hoped would take place in Nigeria someday. Even when the Soviet Union disintegrated, he argued that it was Mikhail Gorbachev who failed and not Socialism that failed. He openly chastised the military regime for staying in politics that the officers were mismanaging. He was a big thorn in the flesh of the military.

* * *

Efeturi was a highly respected man who refused to take chieftaincy titles despite calls for him to do so. He was hardworking and told the truth as he saw it in the community. He looked to Professor Tabunor Orere with awe. To him, the professor was an exemplary child. As for him, with only one son, he would like him to be as educated as the learned professor. He sent his son to the State University, also to study Political Science, the discipline that had made Orere's son distinguish himself as a renowned scholar and popular national figure.

Though a rubber tapper, Efeturi did his best to pay his son's school fees to read to the level that would prepare him to be a professor. At difficult seasons when the price of rubber sheets was low, he prepared palm oil to have enough income to meet his son's educational needs. It was a work that wore one out, but he would not shy away from a task that would prepare his son for the position he respected so much, a professor in the university. He denied himself so many things that his mates were doing—getting a chieftaincy title that would make him frequent public occasions and having multiple wives or concubines to boast of his importance. To him, short of starving, he had to educate his son.

Tadafe was industrious and did not disappoint his father. He made his degree in four years and easily took a master's degree also in Political Science from the University of Ibadan. He then came to his home state to teach at the College of Education that was there before the State University started.

Efeturi was waiting for his son to still read and have a Ph.D. He imagined the fulfillment he would get from his son being addressed as Dr. Tadafe Efeturi. Tadafe also realized that teaching in an institution of higher learning he would not achieve great heights without a doctoral degree, and he soon enrolled in an M.Phil/Ph.D. program at the University of Ibadan. He was able to keep his teaching job at the College of Education because there was no course work to be done in the doctoral program. All that was required was for him to have a project plan that he would follow and occasionally consult with his supervisor.

Efeturi was happy that his son was making progress towards the degree that would eventually make him a professor. He would beat his chest when his son would be called Professor Tadafe Efeturi. The name would be a magic wand to bring respect and influence to him anywhere in the State.

Party politics succeeded military rule and the university and its staff became embroiled in a much deeper way that changed the fortunes of many and disappointed outsiders.

* * *

Professor Tabunor Orere attended occasions that made him see more of his people. Weddings, naming ceremonies, funerals of old people, and celebrations of conferment of chieftaincy titles were opportunities for people to flaunt their wealth and good living. At fifty, the Professor saw how lavish some of his people lived. They had expensive cars; they dressed gorgeously and had their own houses. He knew he had the prestige of being a professor but lacked so much he desired to have. *Will I be sixty or older before having my own house? Can't I change the old Peugeot car to a new Mercedes Benz? How long does one live to spend fifty years in penury glorified as activist or Marxist?* He asked himself many questions. He had to change his life. He had done enough criticizing the military that had now handed over power to civilians. He had begun lampooning the civilians from the onset of their administration for corruption. He had to take care of himself and his family.

An opportunity for the professor to be involved in State affairs came with his appointment as the Returning Officer in the State Gubernatorial Election. He needed allowances to raise his earnings to get some of what he needed. He accepted the offer from the Federal Electoral Commission.

Rumors would fly later that each of the seven candidates bribed the professor and he declared the highest bidder of the PPD Party the winner. As soon as the vacancy came at the State University, Governor Sam Temile would make him Acting Vice Chancellor and confirmed him in the position a year later. In that office, Professor Orere became simply known as VC.

What happened under his tenure would be debated for long. Some said he was the best Vice Chancellor the State University had ever got, as if the university was not just about fifteen years old. Others would argue that he only served his pocket and built several mansions while in office.

After his five-year tenure, he returned to his professor's position in Political Science but nursed the ambition of becoming a state commissioner or federal minister. And this informed his closeness to the new gubernatorial candidate, Jude Osame that he blatantly helped to rig the elections against his people's candidate, Onome Ogbo. Osame had been the chairman of the Road Transport Workers' Union in Delta State.

As soon as Osame was sworn in, he behaved as if he had never known the professor or got his assistance to be governor. His first policy decision on the State University was to order the mandatory retirement of lecturers and professors who clocked sixty years, an order which put an end to Professor Orere's fresh dreams.

Professor Tabunor Orere had to live with his people, a retiree, a pariah among them, and no longer acknowledged in public places.

Efeturi walked away from any occasion he saw him attending. He felt the retired professor was an academic plague that he did not want to step near, not to talk of wanting the son he had spent so much money to train getting close to. He hoped his son would be a different professor.

Whenever Professor Orere's name was mentioned, the elders, like Efeturi and Ode, spat, shook their heads, and uttered what must have reached the retired professor's ears:

"Don't mention that name here! He is the servant's slave!"

CHAPTER THIRTEEN

* * *

Any Problem?

IN THEIR WILDEST DREAMS, BOTH Mama and Papa Tejiri did not expect good fortune to smile so lavishly at them someday. In their early sixties, the man sixty-four and the woman sixty-one, they had suddenly been lifted into a new life they used to see from a distance. So, this is how life is, an ebb that shrinks your possibilities and a flow that raises you to the height of your dreams? they reflected. They had certainly been lifted to an enviable height in their society.

For many years they could barely have two good meals a day; then they lived in a shabby one-bedroom flat. They had left their hometown of Warri for Sapele where Papa Tejiri worked for more than two decades at the African Timber & Plywood Company. Papa Tejiri, like his fellow workers, lost his job when the company folded up because there was not enough timber in surrounding forests to feed the world's largest sawmill company's voracious appetite for timber and the world's insatiable need for plywood for buildings and furniture. For decades, poachers and sawmill operators had been devouring the forests of the Midwest Region and parts of the Western Region without thinking of planting more trees to replace the fallen ones. It was just a matter of time for the available timber in the forests to be exhausted, and it surely did to the amazement of the thoughtless and greedy managers of the big sawmill.

After enduring hardship for four years in Sapele, hoping against hope that the AT&P Company would reopen with some reorganization, Mama and Papa Tejiri left for Lagos in search of some other work. Lagos attracted jobseekers because it was not only the seat of the federal government then but also the commercial center of the country. But Lagos had a way of attracting people there and then frustrating them with lack of jobs. There, their condition became even worse than at Sapele after the loss of the plywood company job. They had to pay high rents for the one bedroom, and the landlady was always there at the end of the month to collect her rent. Without any pension from the old job in Sapele, Papa Tejiri was in dire straits. It was getting very difficult to have one good meal a day. They had to take roasted corn for brunch and *eba* with meatless soup for late dinner. There had been days they had to take several balls of *akara* in the late afternoon as the day's only meal. The couple had become very creative in stretching the pittance they had to survive. They had begun to accept their plight as unchangeable when the unexpected happened.

After ten years of extreme hardship, their son, Tejiri, rescued them from their hapless situation. It was like a miracle because they did not expect it. If someone had told them that they would be freed from the dark, damp, and disheveled one bedroom they inhabited in Ajegunle, they would have doubted it. If anybody had told them that someday they would eat well as human beings should, they would not have believed the person. Nothing in their lives at the time pointed to the relief that came from unexpected quarters. And it came suddenly.

Tejiri Akpome had suddenly become rich. His wealth came unexpectedly as a Niger Delta flash flood from a thunderstorm in the dry season. According to a common saying, once money arrives, one sees so many things to do with it. And Tejiri had plans to invest his sudden wealth. He built two impressive houses in adjoining streets in Warri. In Okpara Street stood a duplex into which he brought his mother and father to live. The building perched on an elevated quarter and with its off-white paint attracted every passer-by's attention. It had four bedrooms, and Mama and Papa Tejiri had more than enough space for themselves, as they never had before.

Their wealthy son provided adequately for them. They wore nice clothes, ate well, and looked every way comfortable. All they did was to live a good life because their son also paid them a stipend of fifty thousand naira a month plus the food and cook he provided.

Now they lived in a duplex at a conspicuous point of the street. Now they were proud residents of Warri, not shy residents living in slums and so did not tell you where they lived. Now they proudly described where they lived to anybody who cared to ask for it. After all, one wears ivory bangles to show off one's hands! Okpara Street was conspicuous in Warri, and when you said you lived at No. 48, people saw it when they came to it. It was not unnumbered or numberless, as many homes in parts of Warri or Ajegunle were. To be doubly sure that people knew the house they meant, they described it as the off-white-painted storied building. It stood impressively and nobody passing by would miss it.

The duplex had a spacious balcony up, and it was a favorite place for Mama and Papa Tejiri to relax. They installed five plastic white chairs, two at the center where both sat. They watched the goings-on in their street and adjoining streets from their vantage position. There they saw children playing dangerously in nearby streets—somersaulting on top of tires—and fighting mock battles with toy rifles as they saw in American films. From their vantage position, they saw men and women's fashions and shook their heads at what young women now wore. They cursed modernity as responsible for what they saw as the half-naked appearance of young ladies in the name of fashion.

There on the balcony too Mama and Papa Tejiri could see far from them the slum they had experienced for decades of their lives. In their minds, one should run as far away as possible from poverty. It was so demeaning and inconvenient. They were now relieved and relaxed. The constant headaches both used to suffer had disappeared. They did not lack the basic things they needed to live well. There was always food to eat and leftovers thrown away. They had the type of clothes they wanted and liked to wear. They had the simple things, such as soap, pomade, and perfume that poor people had to do without for lack of money.

◦ ◦ ◦

"Good morning!" a distant cousin greeted both Mama and Papa Tejiri atop their balcony lounge.

"Any problem?" Papa Tejiri asked back.

"I am just passing by and felt I should greet you," the middle-aged man answered.

"Thank God," said Mama Tejiri, as she looked away from the person who had greeted them.

When they first moved into No. 48 Okpara Street, both Mama and Papa Tejiri had been pestered by needy relatives and friends. They had many relatives, since they hailed from nearby Agbarho, though they saw themselves as Warri residents. As for friends, they had not as many. Not many people really considered them as their friends until Tejiri settled them on this lofty place. The relatives and friends believed that they must be very rich, who lived in such a fine house. And they came when in need to seek assistance or outright relief from Mama and Papa Tejiri.

After a few weeks of the pestering, the couple grew exasperated. They realized there were too many people having problems with basic needs that they could not solve with their stipend. At the beginning, saying they had no money convinced nobody who came to them for assistance. Soon, they started to have headaches from the shameless persistence of desperate people, who would not leave after being told to go. It was in response to what the elderly couple saw as unwarranted harassment that they soon began to dismiss whoever greeted them. They made themselves unreachable by now locking the gate to the fence surrounding their house. They believed one could only beg or ask for money from one who was accessible. They could not feed or assist all their relatives and friends, they told themselves. They rejoiced that they had got rid of their headaches.

"How are you Mama Tejiri?" an old friend of hers asked from below.

They now looked down on those looking up to them.

"Any problem?" she asked.

"I was passing and saw you outside," her friend explained.

"Thank God there is no problem," Mama Tejiri responded dismissively.

Soon everybody in the street knew them as the "any problem?" husband and wife. Their relatives also considered them as their "any problem?" blood kin. Friends also knew them by the same appellation.

Those who used to greet them felt offended by their cold and insulting response.

"Do you feed me?" one cousin asked.

"What do you think you are? Are you Michael Ibru because you live in your son's house?" Mama Tejiri's old friend asked.

Soon nobody was greeting them in their high balcony. They were surprised by the silence that surrounded them. Relatives, friends, and passers-by did not greet them as they used to do. When they saw the elderly couple, they looked down or to some other direction, and passed.

Mama Tejiri did not like this new silence.

"Why is it that nobody wants to greet us anymore?" she asked Papa Tejiri.

"How do I know? I am here with you. In any case, what do we need greetings for?" he asked.

"It's not that greetings sustain us, but don't you like being greeted?" she asked back.

"I don't really care. Those who pass by see us and that's enough," he said.

"I don't like the silence," she repeated.

"Do you like having headaches?" he asked her.

"Of course not, but I don't like the silence," she answered.

Mama Tejiri decided to remove the lock from the gate. Let whoever wanted to see them come in, she told herself. Papa Tejiri did not oppose her and allowed her do her wish. However, no friends or relatives came to visit them.

※ ※ ※

Mama and Papa Tejiri did not know how their son had become rich. They did not ask him the source of the wealth that had made him to build many houses around. They had just been contented with the lift he had brought to their lives.

When Tejiri could not meet the deadline for his loans, his bank did not mince words.

"If you don't pay by the deadline, we'll have to seize your houses that you placed as collaterals," they wrote him.

"Just give me a little more time to clear the debts," he pleaded.

"You know we can't wait for too long," they wrote back.

The second building was the first casualty of the bank's tough policy on defaulting on business loans. Even the tenants of the building did not know that their building had been seized by the Atlantic Bank. One Friday evening, notices were posted on their doors that they must leave their separate flats by the next Friday. "Defaulters will not be permitted," a flyer announced on the same doors.

No. 48 Okpara Street was next in the bank's determination to recover its debt from Tejiri Akpome. The Atlantic Bank's General Manager had written to the Economic and Fraudulent

Crimes Commission office in Warri about Tejiri Akpome's loans and debts. The Commission had sent in two of their officials to photograph the building, No. 48 Okpara Street.

Mama and Papa Tejiri were sitting comfortably in the porch on a humid day. It was an early dry season afternoon with the sun blazing. Once in a while, Papa Tejiri succumbed to the urge of taking gin, and this early afternoon was enjoying with his wife glasses of the Schnapps that his son had sent to them.

"This drink is losing its spicy taste," Papa Tejiri said.

"Don't you know that it is no longer imported but made in Nigeria?" Mama Tejiri asked her husband.

"That's true. I am not surprised that Schnapps has lost its original flavor," he said, nodding his head.

"Still, it's better than our *amreka*," she told him.

"Of course, *amreka* cannot be a match to Schnapps," he affirmed.

They were certainly enjoying the now milder but still valued drink and did not know what those men in black suits meant by taking photographs of their duplex. They clicked many shots, taking photos of the building from different angles. The couple put down their glasses to fix their gaze on the men in their grounds.

"They may be journalists and will likely publish our building in the newspaper," Papa Tejiri told his wife.

"That will be nice. God bless Tejiri for providing us this beautiful building that everybody will like to live in," Mama Tejiri said.

"I believe in future we'll be able to charge those who want to take photos of our home," Papa Tejiri told her.

"We are going to be much richer than we are now. Let nobody come to us with their problems pretending to greet us," she said, proud and believing that their home was the cynosure of every eye.

No other photographers came to No. 48 Okpara Street before a series of catastrophic events started to unfold.

Meanwhile, as both Mama and Papa Tejiri awaited more photographers to come to take photos of their homes and even imagined foreign tourists coming to have a tour of their duplex, they thought of wealth that would make them the richest family in Warri. In their imagined status, the Akpome family would displace the Edewors, the Sokohs, the Odibos, the Obas, and the rest whose names had become legendary in Warri.

They continued to sit in their favorite position upstairs. Once in a while they sipped their Schnapps. A few times they placed an empty bottle of the gin on the table as they sat in the porch for every passerby to see them. Whenever anybody greeted them, they turned their eyes to a different direction. When such a person persisted, as if they did not hear well and greeted again, Mama Tejiri asked "Any problem?" in a very cold voice.

"No, Ma. I just want to greet you. I am going to the market," the young lady, a niece, told her.

Mama Tejiri could not explain why passerby had resumed greeting them. It did not occur to them that no relative or friend visited them in their lofty home anymore. They did not want to be bothered by poor people. They had left the low class and would not like to be reminded of it. They did not want to be pestered by demands for financial assistance. Everybody should work for his needs, they now believed.

One of the men in black suits, who had taken photos of the house, came as early as nine o'clock one Monday morning. He entered through the gate that had remained unlocked since Mama Tejiri decided to have it so. The man in a black suit did not greet anybody. He only posted an announcement on three spots on the house walls. "House Seized by Atlantic Bank. All current residents must leave in a week!" The black suit man left without talking to the residents of No. 48 Okpara Street.

Upstairs, after breakfast, Mama and Papa Tejiri thought the tourist industry that would make them even richer was about to begin. This must be the final phase before their house became a tourist attraction.

"Let's go down and see what the man posted on our wall," Mama Tejiri said.

"Go and read it and tell me whether what they wrote there describes the house well enough," Papa Tejiri replied.

"You are too lazy," Mama Tejiri chastised him.

Mama Tejiri held his hand, and he followed her downstairs. They stepped down with the dignity of first-class chiefs, one slow but steady step after another; their heads erect and not looking down. They had the confidence of residents familiar with their house and its steps. Mama Tejiri jumped down at the bottom of the stairs and Papa Tejiri did the same to show that, though slightly older, he was as agile as his wife.

They were dumbstruck by what they read on the posters. Could this be true?

"I have to read this with my glasses," Papa Tejiri said.

"Let me hurry up to bring them," Mama Tejiri said in a loving tone.

She came back with the old pair of glasses that Papa Tejiri rarely used but made him look so avuncular. He used the edge of his wrapper to clean the glasses and put them on. He stared at the poster. It was what he had already read, even though now magnified into bolder characters.

Was this not a fraud? After all, Nigerians were so smart that they tricked people from their own property? Could this not be the 419 type of fraud that radio and television presenters talked so much about and warned people against?

"It's only Tejiri who can answer this," Papa Tejiri said.

"How can we reach him very soon since he is away on a business trip?" Mama Tejiri asked.

Mama Tejiri decided to lock the gate to stop anybody from coming in to post any more bills on their house walls. She went up and came down with a heavy lock they had never used for the door before now. They had to keep out fraudsters from their home.

Things were getting very tight for Tejiri and he had to be close to his home. He came back from his business travel two days later. His parents sent for him and he came. The father brought him into the parlor, out from the porch where Tejiri had wanted to sit. The parlor appeared to have taken a dark look despite the sun outside. The son did not sit down before his parents started expressing their concerns.

"Have you read the poster on the wall?" Papa Tejiri asked.

"What is it?" he asked back.

"Atlantic Bank is seizing this house. Is it true, and what really happened?" his father asked him.

"If they are seizing the house, it is true," Tejiri told his parents.

"We are as good as dead!" Mama Tejiri shouted, lifting her hands up in the air.

"Why should this happen to us?" Papa Tejiri asked.

"Take it easy. That's life," Tejiri pleaded with his parents.

* * *

The Catholic Church took pity on Mama and Papa Tejiri after they were evicted from No. 48 Okpara Street. They had no friends or relatives to go to. The Church could not look on while two of its members, and old for that matter, suddenly became homeless. It was a pathetic sight to see the two abandoned in the open in the rainy season, their belongings in black polythene bags. The Social Welfare Committee of the Church acted promptly by renting a one-bedroom flat for them in an area of Warri that Mama and Papa Tejiri would not like to mention as where they lived. Their cook and monthly allowance were gone. Their son had disappeared and nobody knew where he was. Rumor and gossip said he traveled out of the country to avoid being jailed for economic fraud offenses.

For weeks and months Mama and Papa Tejiri barely left their new home. Their headaches had returned. They could not believe that they had come down so low within such a short time. When time had made their new status a compulsory badge they had to wear, they ventured out more often. They often felt like leaving the heat and dirty surroundings of their new home to have fresh air outside. In the process, they met people—relatives and friends.

It was their turn to receive the type of shock they had inflicted upon others.

"Good morning, my son," Mama Tejiri greeted a nephew as he alighted from his car to go into the church.

"Any problem?" he asked, as if he did not know her, and went straight into the church.

Both Mama and Papa Tejiri remained silent. They realized the irony of the situation. They went into the church to pray for God's forgiveness and mercies.

CHAPTER FOURTEEN

* * *

Morning Walk

ADE DID NOT MISS HIS early morning summer walk. He had decided a long while ago that he needed to exercise in an inexpensive way by walking in his neighborhood rather than enroll in a gym or buy some fanciful indoor exercise machine. Walking, he had read and heard on many occasions, was the simplest form of exercise to keep fit without strain. Why pay for what you can get free? he asked himself. And he preferred the fresh outdoor air to the stale indoor air of the gym or exercise club. To him, having a tread mill at home would make him not push himself as much as he would in going outside. He saw complacency as a seducer and threat to good habits and he did not want to compromise his will.

Now that he had embraced walking like a passion, every morning he walked along the neighborhood streets. If there was a sidewalk, he took it, but where there was none, he took the left-hand side of the road, walking almost at the tar's edge and facing oncoming vehicles. In this manner, he tried to keep safe in his daily rounds with so many vehicles passing him both ways.

It took him more than a week of walking daily to settle on his route. He had taken some lanes to their dead ends. He had taken some streets that meandered up or down through areas he did not like to take a second time. By elimination of some drives, lanes, and streets, he settled on a five-kilometer route from his home and back.

In the course of the daily walks, he got to know the people, dogs, and the landscape very well. He knew those people who got up early, those who sat in their front porches to enjoy the fresh breeze of dawn. He knew the parents who accompanied their children to the bus-stop so early in the morning. He knew what to expect almost all over the neighborhood in the course of his walk.

He knew, from his experience, that many others he did not see saw him. He knew that his neighbors were very observant and inquisitive. He had met at a supermarket a cashier who greeted him and told him that she wished she had the time and the zeal to walk daily, especially in the morning, as he did.

"You can, if you have to, like me," he told the cashier.

"I know I need it but won't have the time," she replied.

"If you have the will, you'll create the time somehow," Efe advised.

"Thanks. I think I have to try harder. My blood pressure is shooting up and the doctor wants me to do something about it before it hurts me irreparably," she said.

"If I were you, I would listen to the doctor," Efe told her.

Efe knew the dogs that barked and the ones that did not. He knew those dog-owners who walked their dogs in the morning and those that kept their dogs in prisons of fenced lots. He knew the different breeds of dogs in the neighborhood—pit bull, German shepherd, Dalmatian, Rottweiler, spaniel, Chihuahua, Alsatian, and other unfamiliar breeds. There were dogs he saw in the neighborhood that did not look like regular dogs; they must be very strange breeds indeed. He saw how the smallest dogs made the most intimidating noises but retreated once he raised the stick he carried. He saw old dogs lying in their lots and not barking at all.

One resident trained ferocious dogs that kept guard of the compound that bore at its edge the inscription of "Invisible Fence." The dogs did not get out of the invisible fence that ended just by the sidewalk. Efe believed the dogs would tear to pieces anybody that encroached on their owner's property, and so kept away from the sidewalk that passed there. He preferred to walk along the road there and, after, enter the sidewalk again. For most dog-owners, he wondered whether the pet was not a nuisance from the barking whenever anybody passed by. How could somebody have a sound sleep with the loud barking? But the people had their choices, and many loved dogs because they were their best friends, he realized.

If Efe did not do the walk early in the morning, he felt something missing from his body and he would jump out of bed or abandon whatever he was doing to put on his T-shirt, trousers, and walking shoes, and move. It had become a challenge to his will, a test of his ability to live as a disciplined man. Nothing dampened his zeal for the morning walk. If he could not take a walk every morning, and he had the time, what else could he do? he asked himself. He had to dispel his fear of weakness. The walk was no longer a mere exercise to stay healthy in body and spirit, but a means of regulating his life in a disciplined manner. His life hinged on doing the walk daily or he would slack in every other thing he determined to do, he feared.

One very early morning Efe passed a woman. She appeared to be on her way to a bus stop. She carried a big bag and wore an overcoat over her dress. Out so early, he believed, she must be on her way to work. In subsequent mornings, he saw the same lady pass him as he was on the return leg of his walk. That was the stretch as he descended a small hill and walked faster. That was where a dog barked from its fenced lot at him. He wondered why that dog barked every day he passed there. Were dogs not supposed to sniff people's scents and leave them alone once they were familiar with the person? When was that dog going to leave him to pass in peace?

As an experienced walker, he took the left hand side of the road; the woman took the right hand side, and he often gave way to her on the narrow sidewalk. She always wore a mild perfume that he got used to and expected when she passed him.

Efe was intrigued by this lady who walked every workday to take a bus in a neighborhood that did not have a bus route and so had to go far to catch one. She had unique features that made her so different in the area. Her long dark dreadlocks, special dress, necklace of cowries, gracefulness, and other features made her a stranger to the area. From his observation, black women in the multiethnic neighborhood were different; they had their hair Jerry-curled and often wore Walmart or Sears dresses. The women of the neighborhood did not walk with the catwalk gait of this newcomer. He had been in the area for fourteen years and knew the types of men and women around. This stranger was mature and had a certain exotic look in her appearance. Her dark eyes glittered even in the half light of early dawn.

There was a dog incident one day and he had to chase away with his stick the dog barking ferociously at her. She was shaken by the ferocity of the dog, but still said "Thanks" to Efe. That was the first time they had spoken to each other. Her accent was sexy and foreign.

With the daily silence broken, they started a conversation as to why one should carry a stick in case of loose dogs.

"Some of these dogs are dangerous and a stick keeps them away," Efe told her.

"Maybe I should be carrying a stick, especially in the morning. At least by the time I am coming back from work, the place is busier and the dogs are in," she explained.

"I think you need a stick to ward off loose dogs," Efe advised.

"It never occurred to me before now that I could be attacked by a fierce dog early in the morning. I'll get a stick at least to feel safer," she said.

That incident generated something both shared—walking along the streets that, except for both of them, only cars passed. After that incident, they started to greet each other regularly.

Driving home one evening, Efe saw the woman coming home. She recognized him, which surprised him because they always met in the half-light of early dawn. She must have a very keen eye, he told himself. She knew his features despite the half-light of the early morning. He offered to give her a lift home, which she accepted. In the ten-minute chat, he would learn a lot about her.

"By the way, I am Efe," he introduced himself.

"I am Therese."

"You have a beautiful name," Efe complimented.

"And yours too!"

"Thanks!"

They shook hands and looked at each other, as if studying the other to fully recognize the other when they met again.

"I don't really like this morning walk you know. It's because I just have to do it to catch the bus," Therese said.

"The morning walk must be better because it is cooler then than in the afternoon," Efe said.

"Don't even talk about the evening walk from the bus stop! I bet you, it is a drag. By then I am already exhausted by over eight hours of office work and the long bus ride and still have to walk another twenty minutes or so to my house," she told Efe.

"You have to do what you have to do," Efe replied, not really knowing what to say next.

"I barely have time to bathe and eat sometimes," she said. "I just crash into the bed and I am gone till the next morning."

Efe also learned that she had just bought the pink house, where she lived, and her car had been involved in a wreck and so decided to walk and take the bus until she was financially strong enough to buy a brand-new car.

"I know it will take me a long time to put good money down for a nice car, but I have to do so. I hate used cars," she said.

"Of course, there's no better car than a brand-new one,"
Efe told her.

* * *

Every morning, Efe and Therese had their one-minute exchange as they slowed down to greet and exchange a few words.
He looked forward to seeing her and now had one more reason
to feel compelled to do the morning walk. He believed that she
would also be expecting to meet him and have the brief chat
before she continued on to take the bus to work. There was
something in that woman he could not yet grasp, but he wanted
to exchange some words with her every workday. He had some
feeling towards that woman that he himself could not understand. There was something about her that he felt was unknow-
able and yet he did not know why he felt so.

Each day soon unraveled a piece of the mystique that held
Therese in her special class. She had a rich past.

"I lived in Syracuse in Upstate New York for many years.
When I divorced my husband, I moved to Brooklyn, New York.
I also lived in The Village; it was so exciting there, but I couldn't
live there for long."

Efe did not ask her any questions about her married life,
what caused her divorce, and the reasons for changing homes in
different parts of the state or of the same city. He felt she would
tell him if she wanted him to know that about her.

"I have a grandchild and my son brings him in every weekend for several hours. I really cherish those hours," she said.

Therese did not look old, but many relatively young
women were grandmothers, and Efe was not too surprised by
her disclosure.

He was surprised though that she so much liked the arts.
That made her really unique in the neighborhood. How many
people in their conversations talked about the arts in the Birnam
Wood area?

"I used to visit different galleries and exhibitions in New York. I made it a must to visit the Metropolitan twice a year. I couldn't have a good weekend without attending Broadway or a good movie. Now I don't have time to see things. Are there good galleries in town?" she asked.

"They are mainly in the Noda District. That's the area where Davidson crosses 36th Street. Of course, there are a few museums that could be of interest to you too, especially the Mint, the Museum of the New South, and the Afro-American Cultural Center," Efe told her.

"I surely have to explore what this city has to offer," she said.

"Little by little you'll get to know what's available," Efe added.

On another morning, she talked of her Caribbean background.

"My parents came from Haiti. I was brought as a baby, but I still consider myself Haitian in spite of everything."

Efe knew she derived from a stock outside of the United States. Her accent was proof of her difference. He was surprised though that she had not acquired any American accent for all those years from her childhood till now. She did not talk as a New Yorker with a Yankee accent nor was she talking as a Southerner with a drawl either.

Another morning, Efe discovered she had international interests.

"I have a friend in Jo'burg. I like Africa and hope to visit one day."

"That's interesting. You can always visit Nigeria or any-where else in Africa sometime," Efe replied, as if inviting her to his native country.

"I'll take you up on that someday," Therese told him.

"Just let's arrange it, and it will be fine with me," Efe said.

Another morning brought out the interest in poetry and his offer of a book of poems.

"I write poetry, but don't share my poems with anybody. I just write about intimate experiences and put them aside. Someday I will share them with someone, but I don't really know when and with whom."

Efe hoped he would be that person she would share her poems with. It would always be a pleasure reading her poems, he felt without saying it out. He would wait till she decided with whom to share her poems. She might like his poems and might like to reciprocate his gesture of giving her his poems to read, Efe thought.

Efe looked forward to that early morning meeting and the one-minute talk. Perhaps, Therese did the same. He realized that he had not missed a morning walk since the dog incident. No early morning drizzle stopped him from the walk, which had become a tryst with a fascinating woman. One morning they exchanged phone numbers. That evening Efe called her and they started calling each other after work.

"Friday evening and Saturday till sundown are special times for me," Therese told Efe, who wondered why.

"That's my time of worship. I consider myself an Israelite and honor the Sabbath," she explained.

Efe did not consider his lack of a serious religion important enough to tell her about. He saw himself as a secular-minded person who feared God and treated others as he would like to be treated.

Another morning revealed the interest in foods.

"I take mainly fish," she said.

"I do the same," Efe added.

"I don't eat American beef and poultry. They feed the animals with chemicals and hormones, and they are not good for the human body."

"I come from a riverine area in Nigeria and have been raised on fish, which I continue to prefer to meat," Efe responded.

"Just beware of the fish from polluted rivers and oceans," she warned.

"It's difficult to know which is which," Efe said, resigned to eating good and bad fish he was bound to buy from the grocery store.

She phoned Efe.

"I just wanted to touch base with you. How are you?"

"I'm fine. Thanks for remembering me," he told her.

"Why should I forget you when I see you every workday?"

"Not all people remember. By the way, can we have lunch together someday?"

"I only have my break time for lunch. Can you come by noon on Tuesday?"

"I will."

She described where they should meet. Her office was in Fourth Street, and nearby the complex of Government Offices was the Bourdon Restaurant. Efe did not find it difficult to get to her office. They took lunch together among many of Therese's fellow workers who frequented that restaurant.

"You look so young. Are you married?"

"Yes."

"Does she live with you?"

"My wife is away in London."

"I understand many Africans are polygamists. I have nothing against it. In fact, one married man has approached me to be his second wife."

"Can that happen in the United States?" Efe asked.

"There are so many things that happen despite the law," she said.

"That's true," he replied.

"The law cannot catch up with everybody who breaks it," she added.

"You have nice hair. I like your dreadlocks," Efe told her, turning the conversation to something different.

"Thanks. I colored the hair black. You can see it is already graying in some areas," she said, as she pointed to the edge of her hair.

Ade was peeling an onion and each layer brought him closer to the nexus of the spice. He did not know what that would be.

*　*　*

The news of the arrest of a black woman in the mixed neighborhood was not uncommon. But when the picture flashed on the television screen, Efe was shocked to see Therese in handcuffs.

Police had been on her trail for the past ten years or so for a series of identity thefts and bank robberies. Local agents were able to track her to her office and home and, on Saturday morning, closed in on her in her pink house.

The veil was lifted.